AND FAMILY
CLOSEST OF ALL

other books by

STEVE ARNOLD

LAST FLIGHT OF THE SPIRIT WALKER

"A powerfully simple story about family... submerged into a dense and dangerous alt-history..."
Shane Portman, writer & director of
Tumble Leaf

Available now on

amazon

AND FAMILY CLOSEST OF ALL

by

Steve Arnold

Chardon, Ohio, USA

Taylor & Wells Publishing
11525 Taylor-Wells Rd.
Chardon, OH, USA 44024
www.taylor-wells.com

This book is a work of fiction. Any reference to historical events, real people, or real places are used fictitiously. Other names, places, characters, and events are products of the author's imagination, and any resemblance to actual events, places or persons, living or dead, is entirely coincidental.

First Print Edition
Copyright © 2023 by Steve Arnold

All rights reserved. No part of this publication may be reproduced, distributed, or transmitted in any form or by any means, including photocopying, recording, or other electronic or mechanical methods, without the prior written permission of the author, except in the case of brief quotations embodied in critical reviews and certain other noncommercial uses permitted by copyright law.

Cover illustration: *German "Tiger" tank during the battle of Kursk, 1943* by Scherl, via Süddeutsche Zeitung Photo (used with permission)

Printed in the United States of America

ISBN 979-8-9908505-1-4

TO ALL OF YOU WHO VANISHED
WHEN I NEEDED YOU THE MOST.

Acknowledgments

Many thanks to Hugh Thomas, whose book *The Murder Of Adolf Hitler* provided much inspiration for this tale.

Prologue

LAYING COMFORTABLY within the marshy lands of central Germany the casual wanderer will find a string of tranquil lakes. Carved out by the massive glaciers of the last Age and filled with their meltwaters, the highest of these bodies boasts on its northern verge a large oval ring, the *Burgstall*—the remains of a fortress erected by the Heveller princes who had used this locale to dominate the surrounding flatlands through the middle centuries of the Dark Ages.

Had one of those intrepid warriors been alive a millennia later he would have marveled at the sleek winged craft streaking overhead just out of reach. Painted black as the overarching night, it skimmed westward like the Devil himself were after it—or more likely fleeing from it. Nor could our Dark Age hero have scarcely imagined the horror causing the low-slung clouds in the craft's path, not a day's ride away, to glow an angry red.

For just over the horizon, Berlin burned.

"Captain Murto? We're comin' up on the drop zone."

The pilot of the deHavilland Mosquito dropped his oxygen mask with its attached mic to dangle at the side of his jaw. There was no need to wear the clammy contraption at this altitude. He was more likely to get smashed in the face by a treetop sparrow shattering his windshield than to pass out from oxygen starvation.

His navigator rattled his charts and shaded his eyes from the instrument panel's lights to look out the canopy. "We just passed over the Riewendsee, Lieutenant," he announced. "Right on course and schedule."

The pilot smirked. He'd flown thirteen missions with his companion, and ever had the man been obsessively precise, and annoyingly redundant in his speech. "Ya know, Trev, I don't doubt your charting skills in the slightest, but I've had our target in sight for the last twenty minutes." He nodded to the conflagration visible ahead. "And 'sides, for the last hour we've been following the heavies in." He waved a hand at the herringbone pattern of exhaust flames visible high overhead to his left. Though it couldn't be seen from this distance in the dark, they both knew from briefings these were lend-lease

B-25 Liberators in the hands of Stalin's 890th Bomber Regiment.

Trev sniffed. "I'm just announcing our waypoint per protocol." He shook the folds out of his chart like a disapproving father reading his evening paper at the dinner table.

"I know, buddy, I know. It's okay." The pilot eased back on the yoke and the throttle, climbing for altitude while letting forward velocity bleed off. When the airspeed indicator needle passed one hundred and thirty, he reached for the instrument panel and flipped a switch.

"Opening bomb bay doors."

Several feet to the navigator's rear and two feet below, Office of Strategic Services Captain Ardell Murto shivered in his hammock slung in the plane's ordinance bay.

"I'd really like to know who thought this was a good idea!" he grumbled to the icy blast that swirled up into the compartment as clamshell doors opened below him.

"*I think it was the boys in MI6, sir!*" came the pilot's flippant reply over the intercom. "*Really seems like a Limey kind o' thing, dontcha think?*"

Ardell growled under his breath. He really hadn't meant to say that out loud for the mic to pick up. But at least he got a chuckle picturing how the pilot's English navigator was taking the comment. "More like an Inquisition priest!" He unhooked his safety line and oxygen hose but stopped with the mic wire in his hand. "Unplugging!"

"Roger that, sir. Just watch for the green light and roll out. Easy as pie!"

Ardell rolled his eyes and pulled the com wire. He twisted slightly to look below, squinting against the buffeting slipstream.

Black. Just black, and an occasional wisp of cloud. *How far out are we?* he thought. We sh*ould see something by—*

But then there it was.

Subtly at first, just a few pinpoints of light, barely visible if it hadn't been for the red light just over Ardell's head preserving his night vision, but then more and more, with lines from his left and right converging into larger trails.

It was easy to tell, at this height, what he was looking at: the blackout lights of Russian tanks. *Lots of them.*

As they passed by barely a thousand feet below, he caught the suggestion of movement alongside. *That would be the infantry... God! There were a lot of them as well.* Then the suburbs of Berlin appeared, covered by a haze of smoke lit from below by a thousand fires. He was taken aback for a moment by the sheer scale of the destruction happening before his eyes, but then professionalism took over and he started searching for a dark area where he could make a suitable landing.

Good thing, too, because at that moment the lights over his head switched from red to green. He sucked in a cold breath, grabbed the edge of the bomb door and heaved himself over the rim of his hammock.

Once out of the plane and moving with the air rather than against it he could hear the sounds accompanying the panoply of ruin: the boom of artillery, the shriek of rockets, the constant rumble and thrum of a thousand engines.

Suddenly there was a louder growl just to his left as a German fighter, surely one of the last ones in the air, blew past him in pursuit of his erstwhile taxi.

He pulled his ripcord and steered to one of the few darkened areas below him, and thought about the last time he saw a Messerschmitt that close...

It had been barely fifteen hours earlier, when he himself had been piloting a lone Me109 *nachtjäger* across the Channel on his way to London.

I

SERGEANT MIKE BIRTWISTLE recklessly careened his jeep down the airfield perimeter road. It was April in London, but thankfully the spring had been unseasonably warm so the snows had melted early and things were nearly dry by now. Even better, the blackout restrictions had been lifted a few days before so even though it was still dark, he could use his headlights to more or less keep on the dirt track that led to the ack-ack guns.

Which was good, considering he needed to get out to Gladstone's crew *now*.

A thousand yards further on, a clutch of men manned the emplacement toward which Birtwistle bounced with such abandon. 'Manned' may have been too strong a word; the

Luftwaffe had not been a serious threat in a very long time and it was fairer to say they were casually marking time-in-service and broadening their intellectual horizons on crosswords and classics of pulp literature. One private had brought a radio and was paying more attention to that than anything else.

In his defense the announcement coming over the early morning news was fairly riveting:

"... And in the latest news, the Red Army has broken through Berlin's outer defenses and are making a last push for the city's center... "

Before the breathless announcer could relate any more details, his voice was overridden by the field phone ringing shrilly at the elbow of the gun chief. He scowled as he turned away from the broadcast and picked up the receiver. "Sergeant Gladstone."

He listened intently for a few seconds as his eyebrows crept up his forehead. "Are ya shitting me? Really? ... All right then!" He hung up the phone with an enthusiastic bang and stood, clapping his hands.

"Right then, you lot! On yer feet! Got one comin' in!"

The loader, stretched out on the sandbags with his chin propped on his hand, cocked his head toward Gladstone but didn't get up. "Go ahead and pull the other one, Sarge."

"Pull the..." He raised a classic NCO knife-hand at his loader. "Listen, Christchurch, I said... "

Gladstone's voice trailed off as he caught it: the distinctive high-pitched machine thrash of twelve Daimler-Benz cylinders firing in measured synchroneity. The other gun crew froze for an instant until recognition and training finally kicked in. They leapt into action, printed entertainment flying like so many autumn leaves as they scrambled to their places. Wheels cranked furiously as the barrel was trained in the general direction Gladstone was scanning expectantly with field glasses.

At that moment Birtwistle skidded to a halt in the loose gravel, blinding Gladstone with his headlights.

"Jock! Jock! Hold up!"

Gladstone shielded his eyes and squinted at Birtwistle as he jumped out of the jeep. He appeared to be waving a slip of paper, and it seemed to mean an awful lot to him.

"Don't shoot! Don't shoot!" he was yelling.

Gladstone peered out from behind his hand, trying to make more sense of the goings-on. "What the hell're ya on about, ya pug?"

"The plane! Don't shoot it!"

"Don't shoot it?" Gladstone sounded almost like a schoolboy told not to open his birthday presents. "Are ye daft, man?"

"No, Jock! Seriously, here—" Birtwistle stooped to hold the paper in the headlamp beam. "'From HQ. At zero-four-hundred hours today a Messerschmitt aircraft will approach from compass heading one-three-five. Do *not*, repeat, do *not* fire upon it!"

Birtwistle looked up long enough to glare at the gun crew for effect, then continued, "The aircraft will cross mid-field, execute a roll and proceed to land.'"

Gladstone's face fell. "VIP, I take it?"

Birtwistle nodded solemnly. "*Very* VIP."

Gladstone spat. "First action my boys've had in weeks and we stand down? Pah!" He spat. "It figures." Then his face brightened. "What if 'e don't do the roll?"

Birtwistle pondered for a moment and shrugged. "I guess then you can have at him. I mean, that *is* the recognition sign."

Gladstone clapped again. "Outstanding! Boys, get Esmeralda ready! Just in case..."

The crew obeyed, though with markedly less enthusiasm than a moment before. Shells were loaded, the plane, much closer now, was marked, and its flight path tracked with the long barrel as it passed over the middle of the airfield, did a slow roll, and banked into the landing pattern.

"Bollocks..." Gladstone stared wistfully after it as the engine slowed and the landing gear dropped.

"Well, that's it for my excitement. Where's my coffee?"

Ardell taxied the German fighter right up to the tower where an unmarked olive-drab sedan was waiting, flanked by dour men in dark three-piece suits and unpatterned ties. He shut the engine down, flung the canopy open and clambered over the cockpit sill. An airfield tractor darted up and was hooked to the tail before Ardell even stepped off the wing-walk into the midst of his entourage, and as he climbed into the car's back seat the plane was whisked away into a camouflaged hangar.

The ride into London's heart was silent, which suited Ardell just fine. His companions were too well trained to waste time with small talk, and Ardell was fuming and too angry to speak. He simply sat scowling out the window at the brightly-lit streets busy with people who were happy to be out from under the shadow of the Stukas at last, and wrung his flying helmet reflexively in his hands.

In time the car pulled up to the posh St. Ermin's Hotel and Ardell was escorted to an upper floor suite, shown the bar, and left alone. He was enough of a veteran to know how things were going to go over the next little while; there would be a phone call to the OSS office on Grosvenor Street to announce his delivery, then concerned parties there would gather their wits and overcoats, then a car would be made ready, followed by a half-hour drive across town.

He had some time.

He scouted out the closets and, sure enough, there were more suits like those that had been adorning his attendants, and in his size, of course, so he took the chance to get a hot shower and into more suitable attire.

Feeling a little less uncivilized, he dragged a chair to the corner of the room where he could see both the door and the balcony. He mixed a drink and sat, thinking how he *should* be relaxed, but wasn't.

Finally, there was a firm knock at the door.

"It's open!" he called sullenly.

The door swung open and a cheerful gent sauntered in garbed in a nondescript gray hat and paletot coat over a tweed suit. He was older than Ardell, in his thirties, clean-cut of course, and graced with a dazzling smile marred only by a single misaligned upper canine.

He stepped up to Ardell and thrust out his hand. "Ardell Murto! My top agent! Good to see you!"

Ardell stood and accepted the handshake but his heart wasn't in it. "Director Brenner. Likewise."

"Have a good flight?"

"No, actually I can't say that I did." He took a sip of his drink. "Messerschmitts don't have a lot of legroom."

Brenner doffed his overcoat and hat and draped them on the coat tree. "You know, I've heard that. One of our Finnish friends told me he knew of a pilot—taller than you—who actually had to reach under his knee to grab the control stick!"

Ardell chuckled dutifully. "Go figure. I guess you make do with what you've got." He waved his drink at the elegant accommodations. "But these Brits, they know how to put on a war, don't they?"

Brenner ambled over to the bar, picked up a glass and eyed it approvingly. "You're right, these are quite the digs. Almost makes me want to transfer to MI6." He poured himself a scotch and gave Ardell a reproving glance. "But don't be flippant, Ardell. These folks have made some real sacrifices during this war."

"Yeah, sacrifices...." Ardell leaned back against the couch and crossed his arms. "Speaking of which... you have any idea what it took for me to get here?"

Brenner stared studiously into his drink. "An encoded radio message on a secret shortwave set? A fuel stopover in Amsterdam?"

Ardell scowled at the sarcasm. "Don't play games with me, Director. You know how hard I worked to get into the top of Luftflotte Four Command!"

"I know, Ardell, but you can hardly compare—"

"Almost a year's work! And then to have to drop everything at a moment's notice to scurry back here, no time to prepare a proper excuse... I'll be surprised if I have a cover left when I get back."

Brenner arched his eyebrows, then smiled enigmatically. "I wouldn't worry too much about your cover, Ardell. The war's about over in Europe anyway."

"Tell that to the Nazis in Berlin."

Brenner took a long pull on his drink, but when he put it down his expression was all business. "You know, Ardell, I just might have you do that."

Ardell eyed Brenner warily for a long moment. "I'm in no mood for jokes, Director."

"That much is obvious," Brenner conceded.

Ardell studied Brenner's snaggletoothed face for a long minute. "You aren't joking, are you?" His eyes narrowed. "You're *not* joking.... What exactly is going on, Director?"

Brenner's eyes never left the other man's. "Ardell, you're my best agent."

"Here it comes...."

"Ever since I recruited you from the FBI—"

"First the wind-up..."

"—you've been top of your game."

"And then the pitch."

Brenner put his hands in his pockets and leaned against the bar. "I've got a big job for you, Ardell."

"'Course you do. How big?"

"Bigger than anything you've done before."

Ardell blew out his breath. "Quit dodging. Sir."

Brenner stepped up close. "Ardell Murto, I need you to drop into Berlin. Tonight."

This time it was Ardell's turn to take a long swig of his drink. "Tell me."

Brenner eased upward to a relaxed stance. "Twelve hours ago, top-level Nazis contacted General Eisenhower's command to negotiate a surrender."

"Not the first time that's happened."

"True, but not from this high up."

"You think they mean it?"

"How do you mean?"

"Do you think they're scared enough?"

Brenner shrugged. "I think they're terrified. Who could blame them, with Ivan knocking on the door?"

"You mean beating it down with a rifle butt, more like."

Brenner ambled over to the window and pondered the traffic once again flowing below.

Ardell turned to follow him. "So, I go in and, what, negotiate?"

Brenner's eyebrows shot up and he glanced at Ardell with a smirk. "Negotiate? Heavens, no, Ardell. Not *you*. Not with *your* skills."

"Then what?"

Brenner eyed him intently but made no move to speak.

"Then *what*, Director? Spill it."

"You're going to go into Hitler's bunker and kill him."

"'Course I am."

"Ardell, I'm serious. I need you to parachute into Berlin and assassinate *Der Führer.*"

Ardell pondered this one hard. "Okay. S'pose I do. But why now? We should have done this a long time ago, if we were going to. The Russians have it in hand now."

"But Stalin's overrunning Germany. We need to stop the war before he gains any more territory."

"But aren't they going to kill him anyway? Is there really a need for us to go?"

Brenner's face took on a pensive air. "We need the bragging rights, Ardell. It'll give us a political edge in the world to come. After the war."

Ardell frowned and his brows knitted together. "Oh, I get it. This is really just to see who gets a bigger piece of the wishbone after dinner."

Brenner reached for his drink and winked. "See? This is what I mean. You have apprehended the situation precisely!"

Ardell nodded slowly and not at all in agreement. "And when it's all done, what's the extraction plan?"

Brenner suddenly became shifty-eyed.

"You have one, right? *Right?*"

Brenner set his drink on the sill and laid a comforting hand on Ardell's shoulder. "Think of it this way. What if Hitler gets away? Slips out to Argentina? Missions dead already..." He leaned in close. "the lives of millions more already in ruin... and in twenty years we could be doing this all over again."

Ardell stared out the window.

Brenner pressed on. "This could be your chance to personally affect the course of the war, Ardell. And the world to come."

Ardell shook his head. "You know I've given up on that whole control thing."

"The hell you have. You're doing it right now."

"It's a suicide mission."

"I'd say the odds are about one in three you're right." Brenner walked back to the door, collecting his hat and coat on the way. "Look, I can't make you go. I won't. But I need you to. You're the one man I have that can pull this off, and I've already stuck my neck out for you with MI6."

Ardell straightened up, suddenly miffed. "What's MI6's problem? Don't they think I can do it?"

"Oh, they know you have the skills. No, it's your motivations. They worry about possible... entanglements... "

Ardell's blood began to bubble. "You mean my family. They're afraid I won't have the loyalty."

Brenner hesitated, then nodded.

"What a pile of bullshit. Haven't I proven myself enough already?" Ardell exhaled and downed the rest of his drink. "I'll go. But I'm going because I *am* the only guy you got for this.

Not because MI6 are a bunch of assholes." He pointed at Brenner with his empty glass and squinted one eye. "But you work on that extraction plan."

"Ardell, you're a resourceful man. You can find your way out, I'm sure."

Once his chute opened Ardell aimed for a dark area on the assumption it would cover his approach, though it also would make dropping between buildings dicey at best. Steering was tricky, though, as wavering updrafts from raging fires caught his chute unpredictably. Luck seemed to be with him, though, and he was able to put down in a square that looked abandoned.

Not quite! Ardell thought as a shout accompanied his impact and a squad of German soldiers approached, weapons trained on him.

"Halt! Hands in the air!"

Ardell held up one pleading hand as he unhooked his harness with the other. The newcomers surrounded him and one pushed him roughly to the ground.

Quick hands patted him down. "*Boah!*" Ardell exclaimed in perfect German. "Thought I was done for sure!"

The soldier searching him hesitated for an instant, then rolled Ardell over and reached in his coverall where a Wehrmacht soldier's identification papers would have been.

They were there, indeed, and his antagonist dutifully handed them over to the squad leader, who read them with a shuttered flashlight. "Gerhard Duch? You're Luftwaffe?" he asked.

Ardell nodded. "That's right."

The squad leader looked to the sky as if he could see anything, then squinted back at Ardell. "What unit are you with?" he snapped.

"*Sonderkommando Elbe.*"

The squad leader's face turned down into a frown as he tried to recall where he had heard that term before. Suddenly his eyes went wide and he looked at Ardell as though he were insane. "You're one of those crazy bastards ramming the bombers!"

"That's right."

The squad leader looked up into the sky again. "Did you get one?"

"I think so?"

The squad leader's face was still incredulous. "Did you jump before or after you hit it?"

Ardell scoffed. "Before! I'm not *that* crazy."

The squad leader handed Ardell back his papers with newfound esteem. "You should come with us, sir."

Ardell took his papers back, stood and dusted himself off. He nodded at the private that had been patting him down. "No hard feelings, eh?" Then he turned to the squad leader. "Do you have a radio? I need to report in."

"No, sir. Nearest radio is that way." He pointed back toward the city center.

Ardell nodded. "Then I'm going that way."

"Just as you want. So are the Reds." He turned away and led his men over a pile of rubble spilled out from a storefront as Ardell stepped off in the other direction.

Suddenly gunfire erupted from the storefront, the steady clacking of German machine pistols contending with the deadly zipper of Russian papashas, as angry incoherent shouts sounded above it all.

Ardell hit the dirt as rounds pinged overhead. A stick grenade landed on the ground a few inches from his face. He reflexively grabbed it and flung it back into the building.

There was a muffled explosion, followed by a quick double blast, and then total silence. Ardell panted for breath and rose into an uncertain crouch.

A moment later the uncanny quiet was rent by the rising wails of the dying.

II

WAFFEN-SS CAPTAIN Rolf von Heydn put down his field glasses, pushed his peaked cap back on his forehead and scowled. The sky was leaden with low-hanging clouds, but they were starting to clear and that meant the *Shturmoviks* would arrive soon.

There was a muffled cry of "*Fire!*" from inside the Tiger tank to his left. He plugged his ears quickly and the ground shook with the recoil of another precious round going downrange.

This is nothing like Sebourg, he thought to himself.

Sebourg... It had been his first experience with combat, and one of the last the Kaiser's army had fought in the Great War. Only ten days before the cease-fire all of five captured British tanks, sporting large black crosses over fresh camouflage paint acquired from the Belgian tractor factory that had refurbished them, set off at the whistle for the Allied lines. Much to the chagrin of those in charge two broke down almost before they had cleared the staging area. Two more were lost to enemy artillery within minutes of making contact, and Rolf's track was cursed with a recalcitrant motor that left them struggling so badly to keep up with the men on foot that the battle was over before they even reached it.

This, now, was different, oh yes, it was. For one thing he had traded the churned muck of northern France for the wide expanse Templehof Airfield. At one time it had been the parade ground of Prussian kings who had inherited it from the Templars centuries before, until Orville Wright himself had landed his flimsy powered kite here and inspired the construction of a commercial terminal. By the time the war had begun Templehof was arguably the busiest airport in the world and the envy of civil engineers worldwide.

Now the hangars and offices on the northwest verge of the field were littered with abandoned fighters and recon planes and protected by a smattering of Luftwaffe flak guns with their barrels trained low against the Russian tanks. These were flanked on one hand by dug-in Panther tanks from the Müncheberg Division, now out of fuel and reduced to being *ad hoc* gun emplacements, and a handful of thankfully still-mobile King Tigers and StuG III's of Rolf's own 11th Nordland Division. Even though both panzer units had been fairly decimated in the steady fallback before the Red Army, their numbers were still significantly greater than the five tracks at Sebourg.

Plus this time the enemy was coming to him.

The ground was just as torn up, though. It had rained hard the night before and between that and the shelling over the last few days the ground was a muddy morass the Russian tanks were having a hard time navigating. This made them easy pickings for the long guns of the panzers and Rolf stood unconcerned out in front of his line to get a better look at their halting advance.

There were also a lot more of *them*. Beyond the line of T-34's struggling to reach the first runway the ground was a seething mass of Soviet Field Green.

Those weren't the only differences. He had been much younger in the last war, and had entered the army with the full enthusiasm of a crusader. When it was all over the Western Allies had laid all the blame for the conflict on the Kaiser, but from Rolf's perspective the German people had only been coming to the aid of their Austrian kin who had gotten themselves in over their heads in the Balkans. Should they have even been there? No, but one can't always make one's family behave the way they should, and sometimes a relative's foolishness spills over into others' lives. Such had it been in Serbia, and so it had been that Germany had been obliged come to help sort out the troubles. Yes, things had quickly gotten out of hand. But had France, Britain, and Russia been innocent? Hadn't they also been guilty of dabbling in the politics of lesser nations for their own selfish gain? Germany at least had only been trying to help. It was the posturing Allies who had cared more about protecting their material interests, who had chosen to deflect blame by assigning the Kaiser a belligerent motive. They were the ones who had chosen to dog-pile onto Germany, and then cry foul when the latter threw the first punch.

But *this* war... the entire bloody mess of the Eastern Front had been the result of sheer aggression on Herr Hitler's part that had frankly surprised and dismayed Rolf, both from a tactical as well as a moral standpoint. The resulting brutality he had witnessed, on the push eastward as well as the long retreat back, had left scars on him that would be a long time healing. He could still detect the pervading stench of burnt flesh in his nostrils from the fighting on the Oder.

But there was no use quibbling about it; he was a soldier, and that was that.

He looked up at the sky. The only things he really worried about now were the Shturmoviks and his dwindling ammunition stores. *That, and not getting back to Arpke,* he admitted to himself. He reached almost automatically into his pocket to feel the small toy soldier he always kept there.

Not far behind him Private Eemi Becker hunched in the back of the command halftrack and fiddled with his radio.

"This is Nordland Division calling HQ... Nordland Division calling HQ... Come in, HQ, over...." He listened for a few heartbeats, sighed, and thumbed his mic switch again. "This is Nordland Division calling HQ, *over...*"

"Eemi!" Rolf called over his shoulder. "Why don't you pull your SPW around to the end of the hangars over there? All this concrete is probably blocking your signal." He didn't like to burn even that much fuel but at this point it was more important to make contact with Command. He'd heard the Müncheberg commander had fallen to calling HQ with a telephone inside the terminal, but Rolf didn't trust that method was sufficiently secure.

Eemi smiled back tiredly. "Right, sir." He shed his headphones and throat mic and shifted into the driver's seat. The engine sputtered to life, spitting oily exhaust, and Eemi lurched the track into gear, nearly running over another man approaching from down the line.

This newcomer was Captain Bertrand Fournier, a French volunteer who had been CO of the 33rd Charlemagne Division until they had been nearly wiped out by the Reds in Pomerania. The battered remnants of the 33rd had arrived in Berlin just about a week before, and Fournier had been quickly assigned to Rolf's command to take the vacant executive officer position. Rolf was not sure that he cared overmuch for the man; Fournier was capable enough in his role but Rolf got the feeling he was mostly a mercenary who was just happy to get a pay draw every month. On top of that he seemed perpetually unkempt. Whereas most of the SS troopers Rolf had ever met had been fastidious of their appearance, Fournier somehow managed to make even a freshly-pressed uniform look as if he had been standing in the blast radius of a wrinkle grenade.

Rolf turned back to watch the Russians scrambling furiously to bring up a tow track to unstick their rides. He allowed himself a smirk.

Fournier came to a halt a few paces behind Rolf and offered an indifferent salute. "Captain von Heydn? The crews are almost out of ammunition."

Because some military genius forgot our ammo dumps were out there beyond the Reds, Rolf thought with disgust. He lifted his field glasses to the sky again, scanning for aircraft.

"They've only got about fifteen rounds each, average," Fournier prompted.

Rolf ran calculations in his head and did a quick count of the Russian tanks across the field. He didn't notice Fournier's expectant face behind him, still waiting for acknowledgment.

Fournier frowned at Rolf's continued silence, then blew out a sigh. "Think it'll rain again, sir?"

Rolf took a deep breath. "I don't care so long as it keeps the Shturmoviks off our backs."

Fournier nodded, apparently to himself, and reflexively looked to the skies. "Damned Reds! You think the Luftwaffe—"

"The Luftwaffe?" Rolf snorted sarcastically and glanced over his shoulder at the silent aircraft ranged across the tarmac behind them. "They can't do anything. They haven't even the petrol to fly a glider."

Fournier continued to look skyward as he removed his service cap and mopped his brow with a kerchief. "I heard Göring was arrested yesterday. Or turned himself in. Don't know which is true."

There was another clank-clank from inside the Tiger and the track commander called out once more.

"*Fire!*"

Rolf and Fournier covered their ears and the ground shook again. Fournier took a step to one side to look past Rolf and marked with satisfaction the spout of flame that announced the death of a Russian tank.

He glanced back at his CO with another expectant look that was just as lost on Rolf as the last one. After a moment he cleared his throat. "What do you think of that, sir?"

"That was a nice shot."

"No, sir, I meant Herr Göring."

"Oh, that." Rolf shrugged. "They say the fish starts stinking at the head," he offered.

The Soviet formations abruptly erupted in a wall of smoke and the screech of rockets as exhaust flames arced overhead to impact on the far side of the terminal.

Fournier ducked reflexively. "Sounds like they gave up on the field guns and brought the organs in!"

Rolf swept the airfield with his glasses. "It won't take them long to bracket our range. We've only a few minutes while they reload. What's left of our infantry support?"

"Mostly *Volkssturm*. I think we can cobble together one regular unit."

"Do you think they can set up an enfilade position along the left flank there? Use those hangars for cover?"

"Old men and boys. What do you think?"

"Without them to take out the Reds' anti-tank rifles it won't matter if we have the rounds to deal with the rockets." He turned to yell down the line to the command halftrack. "Any luck, Eemi?"

"Still trying to get through to Command?" Fournier shook his head. "You know what they're going to say. 'Stand your ground.' It'll be Leningrad all over again."

"Don't be so pessimistic," Rolf chastised. "There's still a safe corridor out to the north. It would be folly to stay here and die." He watched the Russian infantry finally start across the open ground. The only good thing about all this was that there was no finesse in the Soviet tactics. It was just a wave of men.

The downside was that sooner or later one ran out of bullets.

"We're going to have to try to get the old boys into position. Send what we have over there and tell them to keep their heads down while they're—"

"Sir!" Eemi fairly leaped out of the halftrack. "I have General Krukenberg's staff on the line!"

Fournier looked confused. "Did we change commands again?"

Rolf sighed. "Ziegler was relieved."

"Why?"

"Why do you think?" Rolf calmly watched another volley of rockets impact the grassy sward in front of him as the Russians adjusted their aim. "Eemi! Tell them we're getting pushed back. No ammo. Tell them *no ammo*."

Fournier fidgeted. "Mark me. Leningrad all over again."

"Captain! General Krukenberg says we are to fall back and regroup at the Citadel!"

"Really?" Fournier was clearly amazed.

Rolf smiled at his junior officer. "You, see?"

Fournier shook his head. "It's not the north side of the city."

"No, it isn't. But it's on the way. Forget my last order, Fournier. Eemi! Tell everyone we're pulling out."

Fournier dashed down the line to his tank, leaped up from ground to fender to hatch and slid inside in one smooth motion, shouting at his driver.

Rolf shook his head as he watched. He himself had learned long ago to be careful to maintain three points of contact on the track at all times. He wasn't nearly as graceful as the Frenchman and, were he to try such a maneuver, he would doubtlessly end up in an undignified heap in the mud, and probably hurt himself on the way down. In fact, in his younger years, he had avoided the more athletic sports associations of the NSRL and had limited himself to shooting and, perhaps ironically, jujitsu as a way of improving his coordination. He carefully grabbed the tow cable secured on his machine's rear flank and pulled himself up onto the fender, then stepped deliberately to the hatch and knocked on it with his pistol butt.

Russian rockets passed overhead again. It would not be long at all before the spotters would split the difference and put their artillery fire right where they wanted it.

But before that could happen Nordland's panzers shook off their earthworks like awakening giants and, one by one, started pulling away.

The address of No. 77 Wilhelmstraße in central Berlin had been known to patrons of the arts, culture and science since the early nineteenth century when Prince Antoni Radzwiłł of Poland had used the rococo palace as his personal residence during the latter years of his life. In the days of the Second Reich, it had been taken over by von Bismarck as his Chancellery and, enlarged with a 'modern' addition on the south side in 1930, was further expanded westward down the Voßstraße in 1938 by Albert Speer into an ambitious architectural display of Nazi grandeur: the 'New' Reich Chancellery.

Enclosing nearly an entire city block it featured Hitler's personal residence in the old palace proper, his imposing office as well as those of several government ministries, and gardens, pools, garages, barracks, and an air raid shelter on the eastern side. This last feature was itself expanded upon in 1944 with the construction of a so-called 'Lower Bunker' from which the leader of Nazi Germany would attempt to control his dying Empire.

And dying it was, as evidenced by the battered facade of Speer's once pride-and-joy. Now many windows were nothing more than gaping holes, and the severe carven pillars and plinths were chipped, gouged and charred.

In the Chancellery's abandoned upper-most floor Galya Porishnikov darted down an empty and echoing hallway in the western office wing. She was wearing the skirt and tunic of the *Reichpost* and, despite the harsh living conditions everyone was experiencing, was managing to make it look alluring. Holding her hand and following like a dutiful schoolgirl, Lieutenant Hannah Sommer was a middle-aged staffer who had clearly seen better days, but the look in her eyes hinted that there was at least a possibility for a few more good moments in the immediate future.

Galya stopped at an office door standing ajar and knocked gently. When there was no response, she turned back to Hannah and put her finger to her lips and smiled. Hanna smiled mischievously back, reached up and pulled Galya's finger to her own lips and sucked on the tip.

Hannah shook her hair out of her eyes. "Hurry, Trudy!"

They giggled, and Galya eased open the door.

Dim light from the still-early sunrise beamed listlessly into the room to show it was empty of people and bare of furniture except for a desk and a chair. Wet plaster dust left a layer of pale mud everywhere. Galya scanned the room, then looked back to Hannah and winked.

The older woman sighed eagerly and they slipped in. Broken glass crunched under their shoes as they crossed to the desk where Galya rifled through the drawers to find left-behind papers that she spread over the desktop like placemats.

Hannah nodded eagerly and glanced at the door. "Come *on,* Trudy! I'm so wet! Come *on!*" She peeled off her tunic and blouse, then started massaging her breasts before she even got her brassiere off.

Galya frowned playfully and lifted her skirt to show only bare flesh underneath. Hannah smiled eagerly and her tongue raked over her lips. She waved her hands to the desk. "Go, go!"

"My, aren't you in a hurry?" Galya teased.

"Aren't we all? Ivan is coming!"

"Not before we do!"

They shared a loud giggle, then shushed each other and looked over their shoulders towards the door, but no one barged in.

Galya backed up to the desk, hiked her skirt fully over her hips, and sat on the papers, spreading her legs wide. Hanna snatched the chair and rolled it around to face her, sat down heavily, and laid her hands on Galya's knees, pushing them open wider. With a last desperate moan, she thrust her face between Galya's thighs.

Galya arched her back as Hanna's tongue played over her. Hanna let go of one leg and reached down to massage herself as well, and as Galya felt the first wave hit, she lifted her free leg to where she could reach it with her hand.

Between gasps she drew a stiletto from her boot, and as the second wave swelled she smoothly drove it into the back of Hannah's skull.

On the ground floor near the Chancellery's imposing western Voßstraße entrance Major Helmi Meyer oversaw security for the Chancellery complex... or did his best to, in any case. He was still organizing his space after having had to move from another office that had been hit by a Russian shell two nights ago, and everything was still in crates, boxes, or just piled in the wrong place. He had only just sat down at his desk to review the previous night's reports when a shadow flitted over his paperwork. He looked up in minor annoyance.

Galya smiled brightly and offered her hand. "Major Meyer? Trudy Heffenbach. I'm your new stenographer. Lieutenant Sommer said I would find you here."

Meyer seemed nonplussed at her presence but was clearly appreciative of her appearance. He stood, shook her hand, and eyed the fit of her tunic. "Coming to us from the Post Office, are you? Did the Lieutenant find you there?"

"Yes, sir, she did. She said someone like me was being wasted sorting the mail when it wasn't running anymore and she could make much better use of me here in the Chancellery."

"Mmmm, yes, I imagine she did." His hand held hers and his eyes lingered over her for a long moment. "So, she brought you here. Very well." He waved his pen in the general direction of the front desk. "Go see Lily. She will show you what you need to do."

"Of course, sir. Heil Hitler!"

"Heil Hitler." Meyer sat back down but looked up again as Galya turned the knob of the office door. "Oh! Miss... Heffenbach, was it? Have you seen the Lieutenant? I seem to have some questions for her."

Galya shook her head innocently. "I haven't, sir."

"Well, when she comes in, tell her I need to see her."

"Of course, sir." She glanced at the clock on the wall. "What time should I look for her?"

Meyer frowned. "Any time now. She usually gets here before me."

"Yes, sir. I'll keep an eye out for her." Galya smiled sweetly and sauntered out.

Meyer sat in his chair for a few moments longer, reports temporarily forgotten, staring out the window and frowning.

III

ANYONE RISKING a flight over the streets of Berlin would have been struck by the apparent randomness of the destruction. In some places whole neighborhoods were reduced to rubble by bombing and shelling, and barely a block away baroque apartments could be found nearly untouched, standing shoulder to shoulder like proud Prussian courtesans.

This did not mean, however, that all was well in the more intact boroughs, for within the ever-shrinking perimeter of Nazi territory the beast was feeding on itself...

Several tight-lipped young SS 'soldiers', slim, smooth-faced and still in their teens, hustled a frightened boy between them up the apartment building's basement stairs into the brightening day. The young fanatics wore ill-fitting uniforms conspicuously devoid of decorations one would expect to see

35

adorning their chests given the hardened manner in which they carried themselves.

Their quarry was even younger, and dressed only in shirts and suspenders over tattered shorts. Tears were streaming down his face just like those being shed by his mother and sister at the bottom of the steps below.

With scowls of disgust a handful of the SS boys turned back and laid hands on the boy's family to drag them up, squinting, to the gloomy daylight as well.

Once at street level they pulled their prisoners to a halt before a slightly built man in an immaculate field-gray Waffen-SS colonel's uniform. He had wide-set, narrow eyes that darted about restlessly as he stood proudly in the center of the street before a small crowd of nervously milling civilians. These had been forcibly gathered from neighboring buildings by other youthful members of the officer's band to witness what was about to happen.

The tallest of the SS boys marched up to him and offered a smart Nazi salute. "Colonel Fengeler."

Helmut Fengeler turned from his onlookers to face the prisoners, though he addressed his remarks to the former. "People of Berlin! Know you today that it is the duty of every loyal German to resist to the end!" Though his voice was not overly loud, it nevertheless managed to carry over the sounds of soldiers gathering wreckage and rubble into a roadblock some distance down the street and commanded the unblinking attention of the impromptu jury. "Fleeing the city or refusing to wear the uniform and fight is the mark of a coward!"

He turned on the boy hanging by his shoulders between two of Fengeler's squad. "You there! Why are you not with your *Hitlerjugend* unit? Deserter!"

The boy shivered in terror and fought back a sob. His mother was not so restrained.

Fengeler continued unperturbed and pointed at the boy's family. "Will you stand by while your mother and sister are ravaged by the subhuman animals even now approaching?" His voice rose to a shout as he turned on the mother. "And you! You have been hiding this fugitive!"

The woman dropped to her knees. Her daughter tried to put a comforting arm around her but she shrugged it off. "Herr Colonel! *Please,* sir! He's but a boy!"

Fengeler sneered. "Woman, you forget yourself." He looked up at the leader of his death squad and nodded. "Take the women to the wall."

The dazed civilians, held in check by the guards' guns, could only look on helplessly as the mother and sister were pushed up against the side of their home and perfunctorily shot.

The boy lunged but was ruthlessly pushed to the ground, and a rope was flung around his neck and tossed over a signpost.

Fengeler remained in place, marking notes on a clipboard as he referred to the unfortunate family's identification papers. He then produced a small, neatly-trimmed wooden board, carefully wrote the word 'Deserter' on it, passed a string through holes drilled in its ends, and hung it around the wailing boy's neck. With a nod to his troops the child was hauled kicking into the air.

Fengeler tucked his papers into a satchel, climbed into the back of a waiting armored car, and waited for the boy's struggles to cease. Finally, he turned to the gawking, horrified Berliners. "Such is the fate of all those who abandon their duty, and those who harbor them. Now go back to your homes!"

Fengeler's squad piled into the car after him, and the driver sped down the street as the depleted civilians slowly drifted away.

Fengeler stood in open rear of his car and leaned on the armor plate covering the head of his driver. Behind him two benches affixed to the car's bed carried his steadfast team, hand-picked from the Hitlerjugend units still within the city. He loved his boys with all the devotion of a proud father and was determined they should get the recognition they deserved for doing the unpleasant but oh-so-vital work they were doing.

The city was dying, he knew, infested and infected with the coarse and feral hordes from the East, and it sickened him. Even more so was he incensed by the dispirited attitudes of its own citizens and their unwillingness to do anything to save themselves. *Well enough*, he thought grimly, *if they won't resist the Reds by their own determination, I will lend them some of my own.* Someone had to take a stand, and it may as well be he to set the example and show the listless and the half-hearted how it was to be done.

The driver pulled to a halt as they were about to enter the Mehringplatz. There was a loud roar of engines approaching quickly from their right, but there was too much dust in the air to get a good look at what was coming. He reached forward under the armor plate to lay a calming hand on his driver's shoulder. The column was moving too fast to be Russian; rabid dogs thought they were, even those degenerate brutes would not be so reckless. Fengeler sighed in disgust. These had the smell of home units running like scared hounds.

Sure enough a moment later the column cut across their path at speed: a handful of tanks, assault guns and halftracks, plus a few trucks crowded with exhausted troops. Fengeler caught a glimpse of one of the tank commanders in his turret hatch but was unable to make eye contact as the other man's gaze was everywhere at once and had not lingered on Fengeler's car once it had identified it as friendly.

Fengeler made special note to observe the divisional insignia on the vehicles: an upright swastika with the arms curled into a circle. He'd have to double-check his lexicon when he returned to his office in the Chancellery, to make sure he could follow up with these men and verify their withdrawal orders.

But in the meantime, a flash of white somewhere above him caught his eye. He looked up.

A bedsheet was hanging from a third-floor window, and a face, old and gray-maned, peeped out for only a moment before seeing him and ducking back inside.

Fengeler banged on the armor plate under his hand. "Forward!" he urged. "We have work to do."

The driver put the car in gear and lurched across the plaza. Fengeler kept his eye on the window, marking it carefully so he would be able to find it once they got inside the apartment block.

Just then he caught a glimpse of another armored battle group heading northward a block further on. This one was moving rather more slowly than the first. *So... not running scared, at least,* he thought. *Still, I'll have to remember to check on them as well when I'm done.*

Rolf had spared only a passing glance at the lone armored car sitting in the intersection to his left as he pushed through the plaza. He also had noticed the tanks moving up the parallel street and had been trying to get a good look at them for several blocks. They seemed to be friendlies. *At least we're not the only ones heading in. Someone else is still alive.*

He had to admit to himself, though, that he was still mystified who the other tanks were; the only others he was aware of that would have been paralleling his course would have been the Panthers from Müncheberg Division, but they had all been left behind, out of fuel, at Templehof. Nor was he able to get a really good look at them between the intervening buildings. He had to let that train of thought go, though, as his driver was entering a small market square and it was crowded with people.

On the edges of the space a line of tattered civilians was waiting their turns to conduct hurried barters with a shopkeeper. One by one they would offer whatever they had of value and would then turn and dart away with bags of sugar, flour, and the occasional bottle of liquor. Some would look up at him, standing in his hatch, their expressions ranging from fearful to disappointed to downright disapproving, but none were the least bit welcoming.

In the center of the plaza a gaggle of irregulars was trying to sort themselves into some kind of order, young men with rifles on one side and old men with anti-tank *panzerfausts* on the other. Rolf tore his eyes away from the bleak stares of his countrymen and knitted his brows together.

"Gentlemen!" he called. "What are you doing in the center of this big open space with no cover?"

One of the older men looked up. "We're erecting a barricade, Herr Captain!" He pointed at a tangled mess of bedsprings, baby prams, timbers and random furniture blocking an intersecting street.

Rolf signaled for his tracks to shut down engines and climbed down to speak to the old man.

"Herr Opa," he nodded. "Volkssturm?"

"Yes, sir."

Rolf wondered at the old man's age. "When *was* your time, my friend?"

The old man drew himself up. "Boxer rebellion, Herr Captain, back in Ninety-Nine!"

"Really! China! That was over forty years ago!"

The old man chuckled. "Don't remind me, lad, I have knees to do that!"

Rolf looked past him to the junkyard roadblock. *Not going to keep a marching band out with that,* he thought, *though their medals would surely snag on the loose ends.*

The old man watched Rolf expectantly for a heartbeat, then looked puzzled. He caught one of his comrades staring at him and he shrugged, then turned back to Rolf. "So how goes it out at the front?"

Rolf thought the old pensioner seemed remarkably calm, all things considered. He shook his head and frowned. "Not good. They've taken Templehof. We're on our way in to the Citadel."

"Then they're not far behind you, are they?"

"They're not...." Rolf looked over the motley collection of militia. "Tell you what. We'll help you build your barricade, and then you come with us. I've been told there's still a corridor out to the north, we should be able to get you there, get you out of the city."

"If you think that's best, young man," the Volkssturmer agreed, but by this time Rolf had turned away. There was an excited commotion among the platoon of younger men, obviously Hitlerjugend, who were eagerly pointing down another street at the other tank column.

"Tigers! Tigers! More Tigers!" they declared to each other with a great deal of excitement.

But Rolf's hackles were rising now. *Not Panthers. Tigers?* He stepped deliberately up on his turret for a better look with his field glasses.

The lead vehicle *looked* like a Tiger, and he could just make out the black crosses on the side of the turret, but it was moving slow—he would have expected them to be heading in with more urgency. *Were they just conserving fuel? That at least would make some sense.* But when it turned slightly to avoid a wrecked assault gun, he got a good look at the road wheels.

"It's a Stalin-2!" he yelled. When he looked back at the irregulars, they just seemed confused. "It's Russian!" he snapped. "They just painted crosses on!" He clambered down to the ground. "Tank commanders to me!" He began pointing out positions as his ranking officers gathered in. "Dig in on either side of the street, there... and there. Stay off the corners or you will be easy prey for the Shturmoviks. And don't use your main guns unless I say so. We'll see if we can get this done and still have some ammo left. Go!" He looked around at his other men. "Eemi?"

"Sir!"

"Get the civilians off the street."

"Right away, sir."

"Where are my platoon leaders?"

Several other troopers stepped up. Rolf frowned when he noticed one scrawny NCO with a helmet drooping over his ears. He caught the boy's eye and waved him close.

"What's your name, son?"

"Sergeant Wolfgang Schenk, sir!" the boy piped up with inordinate enthusiasm.

"Hitlerjugend?"

"Yes, sir!"

Rolf looked him over and sighed deeply. "Right. Well, Wolfie, how good are you with that rifle?"

"Best in my class, sir!"

"Of course," Rolf nodded to himself and then pointed to the upper floors of the shopfronts on the west side of the street. "I want you to take two dozen of your best shooters to the tops of these buildings."

"On the roofs?"

Rolf shook his head and waved to the sky. "No cover. Take the top floors. I want you to get into position and wait. When we open fire down here you hit the Reds riding on the tanks, especially the ones with the long guns." If it was one thing Rolf really feared it was the Simonov anti-tank rifle. He'd seen what could happen when that fourteen-by-hundred-millimeter solid round got through a tank's armor and started ricocheting around inside.

"We will at once, sir!" He snapped off a smart salute, but his eyes were nervous.

Rolf returned the salute tiredly. "Don't worry, son. Russian tanks can't raise their guns high enough to find you up there."

The boy nodded and jogged off to rally his squads. Rolf's eye then caught Eemi trying to help a trio of women with a cellar door. Despite his obvious concern they angrily shoved him away and hauled it open themselves, slamming it shut behind them almost on his fingers. Eemi looked back at Rolf, clearly bewildered, and Rolf could only shake his head and shrug. His first thought was, *Why are they still here?* He was dumbstruck. *Why aren't they making for the escape route to the north?*

His next thought was more painful, and really struck him hard like a punch to the gut: *What was that about'? It's as if they hate us.... Don't they realize we're trying to help them? That we're out here slogging in the muck, dying by the dozens so they can escape?*

Why are they still here?

While he could certainly understand the extreme frustration and outright fear of the city's people, he was at a loss why they were directing their anger toward the very men trying to help them.

Rolf shook his head again and turned to face the old pensioner who was hefting a panzerfaust. "Herr Opa."

"No stairs, please, young man."

"Understood. What I need you to do is take your men into the basements. When their lead tank reaches your closest man give it to them, and then get back here."

As the pensioner limped away Rolf just stared after him, the angry women temporarily forgotten.

What was it Fournier had said at Templehof?

Old men and boys.

Wolfie watched carefully out the upper-storey window as the Soviet column turned the corner below him. The tanks rolled indiscriminately over broken masonry, timbers, and bodies, keeping a ponderous pace so as not to outstrip their pedestrian escorts. They had learned the hard way early on in the battle what could happen if that rule was not strictly adhered to.

For the most part the rank-and-file soldiers swarmed around on foot and only a few rode the tanks' fenders and turrets. Several brandished *papashas*, the drum-fed rapid-firing submachine guns favored by Soviet NCO's; most carried standard-issue bolt-action rifles, but there were indeed a few with the long, heavy Simonovs. Wolfie pointed them out to his comrades, wiped sweat off his upper lip, and waited.

In the basements on both sides of the street the old men bided their time as well. The old Boxer veteran had taken the place closest to Rolf's tanks so he could set the attack and watched calmly as the treads of the massive IS-2 drew even with him only a few yards away. *Too bad for them, not using a T-34,* he thought to himself. The IS-2's smaller road wheels exposed more of the lower chassis of the heavy tank and would make easier work of hitting the armor and punching through, even though the plating was thicker. He nodded to his men, tucked his panzerfaust firmly into his armpit, and squeezed the trigger lever.

The warhead struck dead amidships and detonated with a ringing *crack-fizz* as it bore into the tank's guts. Soldiers on foot were flung to the ground by the blast. Smoke poured from the stricken machine's engine grates and flames began licking up from the commander's viewports.

Taking their cue, the other Volkssturm set off their own weapons in a rippling wave and within seconds the Russian column was at a complete standstill. Those Soviet troopers not fast enough to get to cover twisted like rag dolls in a windstorm as the Hitlerjugenden bullets tore at them from overhead.

Rolf's tank drivers and regular infantry then made their own contribution from the plaza, raking the street with machine guns. Rolf was at least relieved he hadn't had to use his main guns—the VS and their panzerfausts had done a perfectly adequate job, and he was sure he'd need those rounds later.

After several minutes the old men starting to emerge from the basements through side doors and shell holes and regrouping safely behind the tanks. There was still rifle fire coming from Wolfie's group, and Rolf shook his head. "Fournier! Get up there, please, and tell the boys to stop wasting ammo."

Fournier nodded and jogged off.

Rolf scanned the plaza. None of the civilians had emerged from their hiding places. *Was it because they were being cautious, and waiting longer to be sure the fighting was over before coming out to check on their own boys? Or were they really turning their backs to us?* Rolf was truly unable to decide based on any logical assessment, but the gnawing constriction in his gut wouldn't go away.

He raised his glasses again and peered down the street. He could hardly see anything through the smoke billowing from the dead tanks, but nothing was moving.

That should hold them for a while, he thought to himself. *A short while, but a while, nonetheless.*

But somewhere in another quarter of the city the screech of *katyusha* rockets challenged him.

IV

ARDELL MOVED more cautiously after his initial encounter with the German patrol, and cursed himself for allowing their casual attitude to lull him into lowering his guard. *I suppose that's how one gets when they're dealing with this day in and day out,* he thought.

Or maybe they just don't care any more...

He ducked into an alley and waited several long minutes to make sure there was no nearby activity. Satisfied that he was indeed alone, or at least unmolested, he shed his outer coverall to reveal the gray uniform of the Thirty-Second Romanian Volunteer Grenadiers of the Waffen-SS and moved back out into the street.

He moved rather intermittently thereafter from block to block as he made his way toward the government quarter. It was raining now, hard, and he was forced to take shelter repeatedly just to avoid getting his only uniform soaked.

By the time dawn was lightening the sky he was coming across lines of civilian women queuing up by public water pumps with buckets in hand. They, like the patrol, stood in numb indifference to the destruction around them and were focused only on their most basic needs. A flight of something, possibly Lavochkins as they were faster and smaller than the Shturmoviks, roared low overhead and the women scattered, but as soon as the aircraft had passed, they returned to the line, neatly arranging themselves back in order. There was no small talk among themselves, however, as Ardell would have expected; their expressions were flat and what conversations there were, were hushed and hurried, and punctuated by furtive looks in all directions.

By now Ardell's feet were getting sore trudging over broken bricks and around shattered glass. Spotting an abandoned car that did not seem as torn up as most of the ones he had seen, he stepped up for a closer look.

It was small and round, and of all things sported a sunroof. Ardell looked it over, decided it was in good enough shape to commandeer, and that he really didn't feel like walking all the way in.

He tried the doors but they were jammed. *Through the sunroof it is, then,* he thought, and scrambled in.

It was a tight fit getting under the dash but after some contorting and cursing—in German, of course, in case anyone was within earshot—the tiny engine sputtered to life. He took a moment to put himself in order, tried the doors from the inside (still jammed), then shifted into gear and pulled out into the road.

Ardell was surprised at the ease with which the little car bounced and jounced over the wreckage. He was making good time considering he was having to dodge fallen walls, hulks of wrecked military vehicles and civilians too-focused on their efforts to survive (which apparently had devolved to the point of stripping meat off a dead horse). Ardell shook his head, sure he had literally finally seen it all, when he turned the next corner and stopped in amazement.

Hanging from the lamppost a small body in shirt and shorts slowly twisted in the wind. There was something squarish hanging from its neck. He stopped the car, hauled himself up through the sunroof, and stepped up close.

He was a teen, at best, and the object on his neck was a thin board. Written upon it in chalk was a single word: *Feigling.*

Ardell marveled, aghast, as the realization of what this meant sunk in. He turned slowly back to the car and out of reflex checked the other lampposts on the street for more bodies. There were none...

... but there *were* several in the many bare trees lining the street.

He was so taken aback by the sight of such wanton self-destruction, such desperate, mindless devotion (if that was the right word) to a perception of duty, that he almost didn't hear a bulky armored car pull up behind him.

He turned and found himself staring at an angular steel door set between two large all-terrain tires. The outline was vaguely familiar and he was startled to realize it was a 247 model—he hadn't seen one in years, and as far as he knew, only very few had even ever been built. *Not all that surprising, really,* he thought, *given the circumstances... the Nazis are probably throwing everything including the kitchen sink into this fight.* He looked up to see who would be driving such a relic and met the heavy-lidded wide-set eyes of a smallish man with a skeptical arch to his brow.

"Identify yourself?" the man prompted without preamble.

Ardell snapped to attention. "Captain Jakob Klugmann, Herr Colonel!"

"Captain Klugmann..." The other man looked him over carefully and suspiciously. "That isn't your car," he observed, to which several too-youthful faces likewise peeked out over the top of the 247. "Where are you going?"

Ardell assumed an innocent demeanor. "Me? I'm on my way to the Reichtag, Herr Colonel."

This time the man's expression seemed genuinely surprised. "Why are you going to the Reichtag?"

"Why, to carry on the fight, of course!"

"Yes, of course." He carefully pulled off a leather glove, plucked up a clipboard from somewhere by his knee and uncapped a pen. "What is your unit?"

"Thirty-Second Romanian Volunteer Regiment, Waffen-SS, sir!"

The man looked down, sneering, noticed a bit of dust on his tunic and brushed it off. "I thought the Thirty-Second were all running west to surrender to the Americans?"

"Not me, sir. I'm heading in. There's work to be done!"

The colonel nodded and swept his eyes over the street. "You're right about that, Herr Captain."

Ardell followed his gaze and lifted a hand to indicate the lynchings. "Begging your pardon, sir, but do you know what happened here?"

He pointed to the closest corpse. "Coward." He continued on, pointing to each victim in turn. "Deserter.... Coward.... Deserter.... Deserter.... Harboring a fugitive.... Coward.... Deserter..."

Ardell fumbled for something to say that would allow him to slip away. "That's horrible," was all he could muster, and as soon as it left his mouth, he hoped it would be taken to mean the behavior of the victims, rather than that of the bedlamite in the SS uniform.

The other man's face became almost sorrowful. "Yes, isn't it?" He looked back down and waved at Ardell's impromptu ride. "Very well, then. Be on your way, Captain. But don't go to the Reichtag. Go to the Chancellery instead, that's more important."

"I will, thank you, sir." He saluted again as the colonel slapped the roof of the armored car and it jumped roughly into gear.

It was about that time that Rolf's battle group finally inched their way up the Hermann Göring Straße to the Chancellery's western flank. Just down the street civilians were picking through the wreckage and rubble of the once-impressive *Allgemaine Warenhandelsgesellschaft A.G.* department store for anything useful, or that could be bartered for needed supplies, seemingly inured to the distant rumble of artillery and recurring roar of aircraft overhead.

Rolf signaled the column to a halt as a guard sergeant stepped out to meet them with his clipboard in hand. "Identify yourselves, please?"

Fournier jumped down from the second tank and dusted himself off. "11th Mechanized Infantry, Waffen-SS. This is our CO," he nodded back to Rolf, "Captain von Heydn."

The guard glanced up but Rolf was staring at the civilians poking through the destruction with an expression that looked equal parts hurt and confusion.

The sergeant looked back down at his list. "Yes... right, then. Captain? Are there any more of your division inbound?"

Rolf tore his gaze away from the refugees and grimaced at the guard. "Are there Nordlanders here already?"

"We have a recon company, a few pioneers, some other stragglers." His face was grim as he looked back up at Rolf expectantly.

"There are no others behind us," Rolf confirmed.

"I see.... You may pull your vehicles off to the side, there, Captain, until you get your dispositions."

"Good enough. Where can I find General Krukenberg?"

"East down the Voßstraße. He's set up his headquarters in a rail car in the Stadtmitte U-Bahn."

"What about my men? They need something to eat, a little sleep."

The guard nodded to an apartment building across the street. "We have a barracks set up over there, sir. You can see what they have, but there isn't much."

"It will have to do. Fournier, see to the men." Rolf lit a cigarette and set off on foot.

Rolf pushed himself to set a quick pace despite his fatigue. He wasn't worried about snipers... not yet, anyway. The shelling was constant but at least it was still a kilometer away.

Rather (though he hated to admit it) he was anxious to hear they were leaving, that the escape through the northern corridor was approved. He was tired, his men were tired, the whole city was tired, he'd seen it on the faces of the civilians he had sworn to protect who had returned his men's efforts and blood with spite and callous disdain.

But then there were the unfortunate souls he had seen strung up on what seemed like every other lamppost and tree on his way in. *That* was a sight that had managed to sicken him, which was saying something after his experiences in Leningrad. And if that's what the people here had been living with...

He clutched the toy soldier in his pocket and pressed on.

At the Stadtmitte entrance he jogged through the sandbagged barricade and skitted down the stairs. The lower platform was dimly lit with randomly-placed oil lamps and cluttered with dark bundles that, on closer inspection, turned out to be fearful civilians huddled against the walls or slouched in folding chairs. Everywhere was the low drone of hushed conversations and the smell of fear, punctuated by dust drifting down from the ceiling with every throb of shellfire.

Rolf paused at the bottom of the stair and looked around. A gritty staff sergeant leaning on another pile of sandbags nodded at him. "Sir! By any chance do you have another one of those smokes?"

"Um, sure." Rolf reached into his tunic pocket. "As a matter of fact, I do." He pulled out a pack and shook one out for the other man, then struck a match for him.

The sergeant puffed it alight and took a long drag. His eyes lit up. "Hey! This is really good!" He took it out of his mouth and looked at it. "What kind is this?"

"They're called 'Junos'. They're from Finland."

"*Finland?* How did you get them?"

"Long story. But I'm down to my last few."

The sergeant nodded with appreciation. "Guess we'd better enjoy it, then." They stood for a moment, each staring off into space, just two soldiers sharing a smoke, rank forgotten.

Finally Rolf put out his butt. "So where can I find General Krukenberg?"

The sergeant brought himself back to reality reluctantly and nodded to a passenger car pulled off on a sidetrack. Dim light flickered from within. "Over there, sir."

"Okay, thanks. Enjoy the smoke."

"Thank you, sir, I certainly will!" The other man nodded his farewell and returned to inhaling deeply with his eyes closed.

Rolf stepped up to the tracks but had to wait for a long train of cars marked with red crosses to trundle slowly by. Once he was able to cross the tracks, he stepped up to the command car's door and knocked respectfully. "Herr General?"

A sternly patriarchal voice answered from within. "Enter."

Rolf turned the handle and stepped in. General Krukenberg, well-built despite being in his late fifties, pored over a map of the city sketched with red lines and arrows. An aide napped in a corner, his tunic unbuttoned and boots set neatly to the side of his chair.

Rolf came to attention and saluted. "Captain Rolf von Heydn, Nordland Division, reporting, Herr General."

Krukenberg spared him a glance. "Ah, Captain. You made it," he observed with a relieved tone, but then his voice became more somber. "So Templehof is now gone as well."

"It is, sir, I'm sorry."

Krukenberg took a red pencil and redrew the boundaries on the map. "Yes, well, it is what it is. What were you able to bring back with you?"

"Eight Tigers, three StuG's, about a half-dozen SPW's. Four truckloads of troops, about a hundred and thirty men in all. I picked up a unit of Hitlerjugend and one of Volkssturm along the way, and I also hear also of our recon company made it in, but I don't have numbers on them yet, sir."

Krukenberg shook his head and rubbed his eyes tiredly. "Too many lost. I fear we cannot stand."

"The Reds swarm like drones, sir."

Krukenberg nodded. "At ease, Captain. Have a drink."

Rolf relaxed only slightly, unused to the informality, but he did as he was bid and moved to a side table. He poured himself a shot and downed it carefully.

Krukenberg studied the map for what Rolf was certain must have been the hundredth time. He doubted any new answers were forthcoming.

"They outnumber us by thirty to one at least, Herr General. It will only be a matter of days."

Krukenberg did not look up. "Yes. General Weidling has been pressing Herr Hitler for a breakout." The general did not seem very hopeful, or even approving.

"I've heard there are still some routes out to the north, some intact units to link up with," Rolf offered hopefully.

"Rumors and hearsay. And even if they are true, can we abandon Berlin? Let these beasts overrun the heart of our heritage?"

Rolf was suddenly apprehensive. "But sir, the Reds..." he stopped, then pressed on as the thought was already halfway out anyway. "The Reds will grind us to dust if we stay... we must escape!"

"Escape to what, Captain? To cower in the mountains?" Krukenberg's eyes glinted in the lamp's flickering light. "To scatter like roaches to South America? Are we not still *'Ein Volk, Ein Reich, Ein Führer'*?" He turned his eyes back to the map for a long moment, but he wasn't looking at it. He seemed to be staring straight through the table.

Rolf felt as if the floor suddenly dropped out from beneath him and he caught himself glancing out the window to make sure the car hadn't moved. His chest tightened and his throat suddenly felt dry. He took advantage of the leave Krukenberg had given him and helped himself to another drink. *What was going on here?* he wondered. *First the bodies hanging in the trees, and now this?* The look in Krukenberg's eyes was... not fanatical... it was *detached,* as if the reality out there on the streets could be changed by staring at a map and moving a few markers around.

Rolf's mind raced through a dozen scenarios of *not* leaving the city, and they all ended the same way. *Did they not care? Was the High Command that ready to throw away their last chance, and ours along with it? Did our lives mean that little to them?* He had known the die-hard Party members were capable of such mindless devotion—he had seen that himself, in the East—but as far as he had seen the fighting forces had always seemed to hold themselves aloof from such displays.

Rolf reached into his pocket, clutched the toy soldier there firmly, and steadied his voice. This was not at all what he had hoped to hear. Still, duty was duty, and he didn't know what else to say. *I never do,* he grumbled to himself. Arguing anything in the moment, let alone with a ranking officer, had never come easy for him. "I see," he responded flatly.

Krukenberg looked up with a puzzled look. "Eh? What was that, Captain?"

"Nothing, sir." Rolf squared his shoulders and assumed a strictly dutiful air. "What would you have me do, Herr General?"

Krukenberg's eyes flitted back down to the map. "You have eight Tigers, you say?" He pointed to a large green swath of ink. "Put them here, on the southwest of the Tiergarten."

Rolf stepped up and studied the map more closely. "Yes. Yes... if I barricade this street, and this one, I can channel them into a fire zone here."

"A few well-placed rounds can do a good deal of damage."

"But I'll need a few rounds to place well. And infantry to watch our flanks."

"I will see what I can do to get you what you need." Krukenberg turned back to the map, but his eyes were staring through it. "Yes. A few well-placed rounds can buy us some time."

"Time for what, may I ask, Herr General?"

Krukenberg didn't speak, but Rolf could see the answer in his eyes. He took a deep breath, blew it out, stepped back and snapped off a salute. "I will see to the redeployment at once, Herr General."

V

IT WAS EVENING by the time Ardell pulled his car up Wilhelmstraße to the east end of the Chancellery. He eased to a stop outside the double-portaled main entry and rolled down his window when two guards stepped up. The first, heavy-set and middle-aged, held out a hand. "Papers?"

Ardell handed his identification over to the eager younger trooper, who then passed them to his compatriot and rubber-necked over the larger man's shoulder to see. "Thirty-Second Division?" He looked back down at Ardell. "There any more of you?"

Ardell shook his head. "Last I saw they were all heading for the Elbe."

"Lucky bastards," the fat one sighed.

"Careful, Hans!" the younger one warned. "You don't want Fengeler to hear you talking like that."

"Fengeler?" Ardell asked.

The younger guard nodded, wide-eyed, and looked around warily. "SS Colonel Fengeler. He's been patrolling for deserters."

The big guard scowled again. "Those poor souls you see strung up all over? That guy."

Ardell nodded in understanding. "I think I actually just saw him a few blocks back."

"He's on his way back in then." The older guard finished sorting through Ardell's documents and made to hand them back, but the relief guard detachment arrived then and a professional-looking staff sergeant replaced the young private looking over his shoulder.

"Evening, Corporal," the newcomer offered amiably. He took Ardell's papers out of his hand. "What have we here?"

"Just another wild boar, Sergeant. I was about to let him pass."

"Yes?" The sergeant studied Ardell's papers with a puzzled expression and nodded back to the guard absently. "You know, let me have this, Corporal. You can get some rest."

"Right, sergeant." The two guards nodded, hefted their rifles, and stepped away, muttering grateful thanks to their relief.

Ardell leaned his arm on the door sill. "Everything in order, Sergeant?"

"I believe so, sir. Thirty-Second Grenadiers?"

"That's right."

"You were on the south of the city, yes? Weren't you overrun?"

"We tried to break out. Most of the men didn't make it."

The sergeant nodded, still studying Ardell's papers closely. "Yes, that's what I heard."

"The rest ran for the Americans. But I came back here to help."

"We appreciate that, sir." He suddenly tucked Ardell's papers into a neat bundle and handed them off to a lanky private barely old enough to shave. "Sir, I'm going to have to have the Security Desk verify your papers."

"Is there a problem?"

"No, sir, it's just routine. Can you pull your car over there, please?" He indicated a relatively clear space on the verge of the pavement.

Ardell complied, shut the car down, and lifted himself out through the sunroof. He was sure the sergeant chuckled watching him work to accomplish that feat but the man's face was a professional blank by the time Ardell returned to the entry. The sergeant waved off the young private to escort Ardell to the security office, and they were off.

The entry gate opened into what was once an impressive and expansive courtyard. This was the *Ehrenhof*, the so-called

'Court of Honor' that Ardell had read about in effusive coffee-table books that had seemed an obligatory element of office dressing in every Nazi command he had ever worked in. The far end was dominated by massive doors nearly three stories high that led into the building's actual interior. In the Party's glory days these doors had been flanked by massive classic-hero style statues representing the Wehrmacht on one side, and the Nazi Party on the other.

Now, though, the sculptures were gone, no doubt melted down for the war effort. Ramparts of sandbags and parked armored cars manned by gaunt, sunken-eyed soldiers had taken their place.

The young private set a quick pace along the edge of the open space, constantly checking over his shoulder for roving Soviet aircraft until they reached the towering doors and entered.

Ardell's excitement to see the sterile opulence of the Chancellery's famous Mosaic Hall was frustrated when the young trooper turned aside and led him up a stairwell to the third floor. They marched down a hall that seemed to stretch on forever, past empty offices and over broken glass and lush scarlet carpeting still soaked by the rain that had poured in the night before through shattered skylights.

At last, they reached the stairwell at the far end. They spiraled down until Ardell was left on the ground floor at a bland door bearing the letters 'RSD' in a hasty scrawl. This was obviously a new home for the *Reichssichertheinsdienst*, and Ardell wasn't surprised after seeing the condition of the top floor.

His escort knocked smartly and ushered Ardell within.

Ardell walked casually up to the counter. He was seething inside about the rush that had obviously been put on his cover papers, but he knew better than to act like anything was amiss.

The private held out Ardell's papers to a harried middle-aged woman seated behind the counter and furiously typing useless reports. Ardell watched as the private waited for a break in her attention, grateful for the extra moments to work out his story, and noted the way the woman's hand trembled when she reached for her teacup. There was a boom some blocks away and she jumped, nearly spilling it on her skirt.

She glanced up toward the window above her desk and started again when she caught sight of the two men. "Yes?" Her voice was both annoyed, scared and tired all at the same time.

Ardell smiled innocently as the private waved his papers at the woman. "Sergeant Manntz said this man needs to see Major Meyer about his papers."

The woman nodded absently, held up a finger while she swallowed her tea, and coughed. "Just a moment, please."

"Oh, take your time, that's all right," Ardell replied. He looked around and took one of the empty chairs in the waiting area while the frenzied typewriter clacking resumed.

He was sure there was a tinking of glass, like a liquor bottle touching a teacup, from the same general vicinity. He scanned the face of the private, but the other man was busy looking out the window.

After a few more minutes there was a ratcheting zing as paper was pulled from a carriage and the woman's face appeared over the counter, slightly calmer. "Private? His papers, please?" She snatched them out of the lad's hand and walked briskly back to peek around the door of an inner office. The soldier sighed and left, and Ardell could easily tell the boy was going to make full use of the opportunity to take the most circuitous route he would be able to find on his way back to duty at the gate.

Ardell sat back down and examined his fingernails nonchalantly. He tried to listen in on the conversation but it was too far away and there was too much ambient noise, between the shelling, small arms fire, and echoing of conversations in the hallway outside.

He looked up at the sound of another pair of heels rounding the door into the security office and was amazed at what he saw.

Or who, rather...

She was tall and slim, and remarkably well put-together considering the circumstances, with a light frilly blouse and knee-length skirt. Auburn hair fell loosely over her shoulders and she actually was wearing lipstick. But what was really remarkable was that he knew that face behind the makeup.

And it didn't bode well for him.

"Fancy meeting *you* here!" he stage-whispered.

Galya stopped in mid-stride and turned slowly to see who had addressed her. When their eyes met, hers widened only the slightest amount, though Ardell noticed.

"Got you." He was smirking to cover up his irritation.

She only took a moment to recover completely. "Well, well, if it isn't my old friend..." She glanced around quickly. The other girl was still leaning into Meyer's office and no one else was in earshot.

"Jakob Klugmann," Ardell breathed.

"Trudy Heffenbach," Galya replied, then in a more normal tone, "Kobus, Kobus! My old friend! How are you? How have you been since Dresden?"

"My goodness," Ardell replied casually. "How long has it been? A year already?"

"Fourteen months and a few days, but I'm not counting, darling."

Meyer stepped around the counter then with Ardell's papers in hand, face intrigued at their exchange. "I'm sorry, Miss Heffenbach, do you two know each other?"

Galya smiled brightly. "Herr Major! This is my old friend Kobus Klugmann! We used to be neighbors in Stuttgart!"

"Did you now?"

Ardell stood. "Yes, sir. My family actually rented an apartment above her father's bakery. You can imagine how nice it was, every day to wake up to the smell of fresh-baked bread!"

Galya nodded wistfully. "Yes, those were the days!"

"Yes, I'm certain they were." Meyer seemed unimpressed. "How nice for you to be able to catch up again."

Ardell assumed an apologetic air. "Yes, well, it is... in spite of everything." He kicked himself mentally, though, when he saw the annoyance on Meyer's face at his comment.

The security chief glanced at Ardell's papers, still in his hand, then looked back at Ardell, but did not hand them back. "Captain Klugmann. Your papers appear to be in order, but I am going to hold onto them for just a little longer until I can get word back from SS HQ."

Ardell nodded amiably but his mind was racing. The SS leadership, assuming his intel was correct, was still in the Reich Security building on Prinz Albert Straße. It would take some time to get a runner there and back, but when that happened Meyer would know there was no Jakob Klugmann with the Thirty-Second Grenadiers. He would have to have a backup plan in place by then, and he wondered briefly if it would be feasible to take Meyer out and be done with it.... Maybe he could get Galya to help, since she had just vouched for him and thereby put her own cover at risk.

No, he thought, *shut that idea down.* A side trip like that could completely derail his real mission. It would probably be more efficient to play dumb and claim his records must have been lost. There *was* a war on, after all. All he'd have to do was bluff along for a few hours until he could do what he came for and get out.

"Understood, Herr Major," he agreed. "What should I do in the meantime?"

"I'm going to put you with your own kind, Captain."

"Beg pardon?"

"Panzergrenadiers. There's a unit that just arrived this afternoon, the 11th Nordland. I'm sure they could use some help."

"Oh, I'm sure! That will do nicely, thank you, sir."

"Good." Meyer appeared relieved to be rid of a minor irritation. He looked back over his shoulder and drew breath. "Oster!"

An older, gruff-looking man in a police uniform appeared out of another office.

Meyer addressed Ardell and Oster curtly. "Captain, this is our Master-At-Arms Herr Oster. Herr Oster, I need you to escort Captain Klugmann here to the barracks. He's being assigned to the 11th."

"Right, sir." Oster nodded and reached back into his office to grab a greatcoat.

Ardell turned back to Galya as Meyer collected the reports from his now-tipsy secretary and headed back to his office.

"Trudy. Shall we get something to eat later? Catch up?"

Galya smiled coyly. "That is very tempting, but it will have to wait. I have other things I need to do first. But I will see you later."

"You can count on it."

"You certainly can."

Oster shrugged himself into his coat, stepped between Ardell and Galya, and pointed a hand toward the door.

The short walk from the RSD office out the imposing west lobby to the barracks across the street seemed nothing compared to the jaunt from the east entry. In addition, the Russians seemed to be less of a threat on this end of the block. It was remarkable, Ardell thought, how hit-and-miss things were. It was like seeing a tornado back home that would take out an entire line of houses and leave a barn untouched on the opposite side of the road, or the time he had been in Hawaii and it had rained on one end of his hotel and not the other.

The barracks were lit by oil lamps and hand-cranked *taschenlampen*. A few queries of random soldiers scurrying about on their own urgent affairs soon led them to a rumpled-looking Frenchman named Fournier who very politely explained that no, their CO was not present, he had just returned from a meeting with their sector commander and had left to get something to eat in the officer's mess in the Chancellery.

Oster looked frustrated and led Ardell to a window looking out onto the Hermann Göring Straße. He pointed across the street to a smaller building just behind the west wing of the Chancellery.

"That's the SS barracks. You'll find the officers' mess there." He glared at Ardell for effect. "Go straight there and find this guy. Don't go anywhere else. Understood?"

Fournier stepped up behind Ardell and clapped him on the shoulder. "How about I just take him over there? I need a little something for myself anyway."

Oster scowled, then nodded once and stomped out the door.

Fournier smiled at Ardell. "So! Thirty-Second, eh? Romanian, aren't you? Or Hungarian?"

Ardell shrugged. "Most of the men were, one or the other. Not me, though, I was pulled from Sixth Mountain."

They stepped out into the street and immediately ducked for cover when a volley of shells hit the Chancellery garden. One round clipped the top floor of the main hall and sent concrete and marble chips flying in all directions.

Fournier got up and dusted himself off, and lifted Ardell by his elbow. "The good news is that since it's dark their spotter planes can't do any ranging. They're just shooting at random now."

"That's the god news?"

Fournier shrugged. "Well, it really means they're less likely to hit you. Come on!" The Frenchman broke into a sprint and Ardell followed.

Inside the SS barracks things were only slightly better than across the street. There were actual electric bulbs running off generators, though the accommodations were more austere compared to the re-purposed apartment house the 11th occupied.

They made their way through more soldiers, who looked just as anxious, tired and determined as their counterparts across the street. Ardell had to hustle to keep up with Fournier, who seemed to exude a remarkable amount of energy.

"So, your CO," he panted as he squeezed past two men luffing a crate of *panzerschrecks* down the hall. "What's he like?" At this point Ardell wasn't too concerned if he was going to be working around someone fanatical or indifferent. Both were equally dangerous in their own right; he just had to know what set of methods to put into play.

The question seemed to draw Fournier up short and he paused for a moment to consider. "Well, he cares about his men..."

"You say that like you're trying to sell me a used car."

Fournier chuckled. "You know, you're right. I guess he just doesn't come across that way. He's a hard one to read. And you have to be very direct when you talk to him."

"How do you mean?"

Fournier scratched at his whiskers. "How can I say this... he just doesn't seem to get hints, you know?"

They entered the officer's mess and Fournier stopped just within the door to scan the room. "There," he pointed. "Come on."

Ardell followed Fournier past the counter where tired cooks dished out dubious provender and stopped behind a tallish man sipping coffee while absently turning over a small toy soldier in his hand.

Fournier cleared his throat. "Captain von Heydn? Got a new straggler for us."

The man turned around and looked up, and suddenly all of Fournier's comments made perfect sense to Ardell. He was never so glad as he was at that moment, that he had been trained in maintaining a poker face no matter what.

For the man sitting at the table was the very embodiment of Brenner's concerns—Ardell's father, Rolf von Heydn.

VI

IN THE FALL of 1935 Ardell had been a dutiful student at a small secondary school just outside of the little burg of Arpke. His father Rolf was a math professor there, which was how he could afford to go. Times were still very tough—the Nazis had only just taken over from the Weimar government two short years before and the country was still recovering from the old Republic's disastrous economic policies.

Ardell had been something of an anomaly at the school, born of a German father and an American mother. It was quite a story how they had met: Rolf had mustered out of the Kaiser's infant tank corps with the Armistice and after drifting about rudderless for a time found himself almost by accident in the *Freikorps'* Iron Brigade in Latvia. Wounded and recovering in a British aid station he had met Margaret Murto, an American nurse, and when he was released, they returned to his homeland in Hanover and settled down to have a family.

Life was, at best, 'quaint', which meant housing was cramped and money was short. Ardell remembered never having the wherewithal to do much of anything, but then, neither did anyone else back then. The general discontent of paying back reparations while rebuilding a shattered country made Germany a hotbed of conflict between dozens of paramilitary groups. On the one side were the fragmented remains of the Freikorps (who were still stinging from the defeat in the Great War and wanted nothing more than to get some of their old reputation back) while on the other were the communists who were pushing a borderless solidarity among the working class. Ardell came of age during this time and, for a while, took a keen interest in their rhetoric, but the only sense he was able to make out of it all was that 'national' socialists were still socialists, just like the communists, the only difference being they were limiting their favors to their own kinfolk.

This was a feeling he knew he had inherited from his mother. Having served in the East she had a soft spot in her heart for the victims of Bolshevism. She had broken out in tears when she had heard of the genocidal pogroms inflicted by Stalin on the citizens of the Ukraine when he confiscated all their grain and left tens of millions to die.

Then the Nazis took control. Ardell's father, ever a rather desperate optimist, had tried to look on the bright side: the economy is a wreck, and isn't Herr Hitler promising a better life? Hadn't Mussolini, who had been at this longer, managed to finally resolve trade disputes in his own country? Even the notoriously inefficient Italian rail system was finally running on time.

Then came the day Rolf had had to make a choice. Ardell recalled it all too well—he had just turned fifteen and his father had come home from the school looking pale and edgy. The Nazis had started building up the military in open defiance of the Armistice and representatives from the Wehrmacht had been meeting with school staff about their experiences as veterans of the War. Rolf was to have an interview the following day, and he knew they would pressure him to join the new panzer corps.

Ardell's mother had nearly dropped dinner on the floor. She begged him to hide his background, even going so far as to suggest they leave for the US and stay with her family until they got reestablished. She was clearly worried about where Hitler's ambitions would take the country and didn't want her sweet Rolf getting caught up in the fervor. But Rolf seemed stuck, as if afraid. It wasn't until much later that Margaret explained to her son what happened, that leaving a wrecked Germany for an unknown Baltic had been traumatic for Rolf in 1919. He couldn't stomach doing it again. But staying and covering up his past was likewise no good since he was sure they would just search his records, find where he had served, and then make life very difficult for him. All he felt he could do was go through with the interview and give up his teaching job for the military.

It was all very calm and sensible hearing this in his grandmother's sitting room in Cleveland as an adult, but at the time Ardell only remembered the huge row that had ended with he and his mother packing their things, and his father standing stone-faced in the doorway fidgeting with one of Ardell's childhood toy animals as they left. Whether or not Rolf had been hurt by the piece of his mind Ardell had given him about his inability to stand up to a bunch of goose-steppers, Ardell had figured he would never know. And he hadn't been sure, on that day, that he had even cared to.

It was clear Fournier had been too focused on getting himself something to relieve the gnawing in his gut to notice the look on Rolf's face. Ardell had registered Rolf's amazement immediately, though, and thrust out his hand.

"Klugmann! Captain Jakob Klugmann. Thirty-Second Grenadiers! Call me Kobus!"

Several other patrons looked up briefly at the loud disturbance before sullenly returning to their meals. When

Rolf didn't respond to Ardell's handshake, he sat heavily across from his father, mind racing.

The mission was over. It was that simple. It wasn't just that Rolf knew who he really was, it was that Ardell didn't know that his father wouldn't turn him in. After all, they had not parted on good terms and the last Ardell knew Rolf's sleeves were getting fitted for fylfot flashes.

The real trouble now was that he had to get out of the city before the man sitting across the table from him could decide to turn him in.

Rolf studied Ardell closely over his coffee but, as always, his face was flat as a marble slab and Ardell couldn't tell what he was thinking.

There was a muffled boom somewhere overhead and dust drifted down from the ceiling. Rolf set his cup down and covered it with his hand.

"Well..." There was a long pause, and Ardell was sure Rolf had caught himself before using his son's real name. "I have to admit, I never expected to see you here."

"Up until yesterday neither did I."

Rolf nodded, watching Ardell without making eye contact, and fidgeted with the toy soldier in his hand. "May I ask how you came to be—"

"I'm just here taking in the sights."

Rolf squinted up at the ceiling and seemed to nod to himself before lifting his cup to his lips again. "Of course."

His next words were in a more appropriate whisper. "Last I knew you were FBI."

"So, you *were* paying attention."

"I'm guessing now you must be—"

"Let's just say I'm making sure the Michelin guide is going to be up to date. Lots of new changes around here lately."

Rolf seemed genuinely puzzled at this and Ardell recalled he never had been one for sarcasm. When he did speak his voice carried a note of some wonder. "You've become a smart-ass in your maturity. You used to be very straight-and-narrow. Even obsessive."

"I'm not the kid I used to be. I realized life is too short to not laugh when you have a chance."

"Not something I would have expected... from my son."

"So you *are* claiming me. Does that mean you aren't going to turn me in?"

"Should I?"

"It's your duty."

"Your mother would never forgive me."

"I'm surprised that bothers you."

"Is she still that mad at me?"

"She can carry a grudge like it's got a handle. But what do you think? You stayed behind and took up with... Ilse? Was that her name?"

"Let's not drag that up again."

"Oh, no. Not here. This isn't the place." Ardell leaned back and took a deep breath. "What's that in your hand? Is that Dieter's?" Ardell was angry, and getting angrier, and knew he had to shut that down or he would never get out... but he just kept playing the scene in his head over and over, of Rolf sanding in the doorway with a small toy of *his,* and now it felt like he had been replaced by Ilse's child whom he'd never even met. "Look. There's only one thing I need from you, and it's exactly *nothing*. Not a word, not a look, not a hint to your Nazi heroes. You and I stay clear of each other until I'm gone. That should be pretty easy for you, right?"

Rolf stared at him for another long moment with that infuriatingly bland expression, and finally let out a breath Ardell hadn't realized the man had been holding. What he said next, Ardell had to admit, caught him completely off guard.

"And just how would you know what's easy for me?"

Ardell felt like he had just lost control of the discussion. He figured that was as good an indicator as any that their chat was over. "Whatever. Just stay out of my way."

Ardell pushed his way out of the barracks, counting on his captain's uniform and a stormy expression to help clear a path among the rank-and-file. He jogged quickly across the adjacent open area to re-enter the Chancellery proper and ducked when another Soviet artillery salvo struck the north side of the complex by the greenhouse. He wasn't sure exactly where he was going, but reasoning that a recon of the offices was called for in hopes of finding out something about the tactical situation beyond the barricades. Not only that but he needed time to calm down, and time to *think*.

He cursed under his breath, and this time he wasn't careful what language he used. *Of all the people to run into here. Of all places!* he groused to himself. All the effort getting him here, the risks taken by the Mosquito crew, he himself putting his own life and limb on the line, and now this. It was true that he had, in fact, signed up for this in every sense of the word, but the sheer irony that what could have been a real feather in his cap and a real career booster at home, was going down the drain because of one single person who just *happened* to be here.

His own father, screwing things up for him *again*.

Back inside the main building he paused to lean against a wall to collect his thoughts. *Exit strategy... exit strategy....*

Truth was, he had none.

'...Ardell, you're a resourceful man. You'll find a way out, I'm sure...' He drove his fist into his palm. *This is how it is... I get a one-way ticket so Winnie and Uncle Joe can figure out who gets stuck with the bill!*

But Galya... Galya was here, and if anyone in Stalin's Secret Police was his counterpart, she was it. He could easily guess why she was here—almost certainly for the same thing he was, just for different reasons. While it would have been a nice challenge to see who would have reached the objective first, and the ultimate result of successful execution, this one he was just going to have to hand to her.

But much more importantly he was certain *she* had an exit strategy. After all, her people were less than a half-mile away.

Somewhere nearby another round of artillery shells shook the floors.

"Captain Klugmann? Jakob Klugmann?"

Ardell turned to see two grim-looking men taking up positions on each side of him. They wore the green uniforms of the *Orpo* and were adorned with service badges indicating a rather more veteran status than many of the Chancellery's denizens. Physically they were cookie-cutter copies of each other, square-jawed and distant-eyed with only a slight difference in height to set them apart.

"Yes?" Ardell answered warily.

"Herr Oster wants to see you," Tall Square-Jaw said in clipped tones. "You need to come with us, please."

Ardell's first question was how a police officer's *want* to see him translated into a *need* for him to appear, but that thought was quickly replaced by trying to figure out the *why*. Could they have heard from SS HQ already? Could a runner have gotten there and back that fast?

Or did Rolf somehow manage to get word to Oster while he was stomping around brooding?

Within a few minutes he was back in the RSD office. Galya was nowhere to be seen. His tight-lipped escorts stopped him at the outer counter and then Tall Square-Jaw rapped smartly on Oster's door. Inside Ardell could hear Oster's voice, and another's he didn't recognize.

"I'm telling you that maniac Fengeler has been commandeering my officers to run courier missions to the Humboldthain Flak Tower! He wants to get Bärenfänger to mount a counterattack!"

"Counterattack!" Oster's tone was scathing. "Against that? What does he think Bärenfänger can do?"

"Who cares what he thinks? The Russians have closed the circle anyway. There's no way through. And I'm done having good men wasted on suicide missions!"

"Okay, calm down, I'll see what I can do with him."

There was an audible exhale, and then "Thank you, sir." There was the sound of chairs being scraped across the floor. "I'll get back to my duties now."

"Of course, Sergeant. Be careful."

The door opened and a tired-looking Orpo *Hauptscharführer* emerged. As he brushed past Ardell's guards they straightened up, took Ardell firmly by the elbows, and ushered him in.

The Master-At-Arms was hurriedly packing files into boxes and stacking them neatly against the wall.

"Sir? We have Captain Klugmann."

Oster looked up and nodded. "Excellent. Thank you, sergeant, that will be all."

The Orpo officers backed out and closed the door behind them. Oster sat back at his desk and picked up a thin sheaf of papers that Ardell recognized as his identification.

Oster wasted no time on niceties. "Do you know why you are here, Captain?"

Ardell assumed a benign expression. "To collect my papers?"

"No." Oster rifled through them absently. "The duty sergeant had concerns about you, and I felt he was justified. They looked a little... shall we say 'off'? Though I couldn't quite put my finger on the problem. I decided just to go straight to the source and called over to the SS headquarters."

So they still have some *telephone service,* Ardell griped in his head. *And Dad didn't turn me in. Interesting, but at the moment there are bigger fish to fry.* "And...?"

"It turns out there is no record of a Jakob Klugmann in the Thirty-Second Grenadiers. Or anywhere in the Waffen-SS, for that matter."

"Are you accusing me of having falsified papers, Herr Oster?"

"Well, it does seem rather appropriate that your name translated into English means 'smart guy'." Oster cocked an eyebrow at Ardell. "Are they falsified?"

"Begging your pardon, Herr Oster, but why might I use false papers to gain entry here?"

"That is really nothing I care about."

"It—it isn't?" Ardell was taken aback.

Oster shrugged. "Herr Captain, I don't care who you are. Or why you are here."

Now it was Ardell's turn to raise an eyebrow. "I admit I'm surprised you could say that."

Oster sighed tiredly. "Don't be. I don't care if you're a spy or one of those foreign zealots like in the Charlemagne Division, just crawling in here to prolong the fight for no good purpose. Either way you're a liability."

"I see.... So what is to become of me?"

Oster seemed taken aback. "Why, I'm going to have you taken outside and shot, of course."

Of course! Ardell's brain shifted into high gear. *Exit strategy... exit strategy... exit strategy...* He still had none! And judging by what he overheard there was no sure route through the Soviets, and Galya wasn't here to bail him out. He still needed time, and a chance to snoop for intel just to get *out.*

But hold on... Oster called SS HQ, so Prinz Albert Straße is still in German hands... and before his assignment to

Luftflotte 4 he was working with the Gestapo, and reporting directly to their HQ at...

Yes! Ardell took a deep breath and smiled. "How soon can we do this?"

Again, Oster seemed astonished. He squinted closely at Ardell. "I beg your pardon?"

"I said, how soon can we do this?"

"You want me to hurry? You have no story, no excuse in your defense?"

"*Nee!*" Ardell shrugged like a rebellious child caught with his hand in the cookie jar. "You've found me out!"

Oster glared at him, still squinting, but in the end probably decided being rid of one less crazy, whatever the nature of their crazy, was the most important thing at this particular moment. "Well! I'm glad we cleared that up." He opened his desk drawer, pulled out a form from a stack of blanks, then stepped out from behind his desk to the door and waved Ardell out.

In the outer office the Square-Jaw Siblings were giving their undivided attention to Galya, who had returned from elsewhere in the Chancellery laden with stacks of files.

"Oh, you're back?" Oster asked with some irritation.

Of course, she is... now, Ardell thought.

Galya stepped around Short Round with a playful wink. "Just a little last-minute filing before I lock up, sir." She caught sight of Ardell and her eyebrows went up. "Oh, hello,

Kobus, my love!" Her demeanor at once was more sentimental and personal, much to the obvious displeasure of Short Round.

She turned back to Oster. "Unless you're going to be here for a while yet, sir?"

Oster shook his head once. "No. We're just heading out. But as a matter of fact, I need you to come with us." He grabbed a clipboard off the counter, clamped his papers onto it and handed it to her.

She skimmed the form's header and her eyebrows went up again as Oster turned to Tall Square.

"Sergeant, take charge of the prisoner and escort him to the garden wall."

"At once, sir." Tall Square took Ardell by the elbow and pulled him out of the office. "Come on, you."

Outside rain was beginning to drizzle again. The now-nearly-constant artillery fire seemed closer, punctuated by the occasional boom of German eighty-eights returning the favor.

Ardell was marched to a lonely wall in the wreckage-strewn Chancellery garden pocked with bullet holes. Short Round offered him a blindfold but Ardell shook his head. Tall Square then surprised Ardell by offering him a cigarette which he gratefully accepted.

They then stepped back several yards and prepared their weapons. Oster finally emerged from within the Chancellery with Galya in tow, who cringed more at the rain than the barrage, and stepped up close to his men.

"Any last words, Herr Captain?"

"May I make a request?"

"Depends." Oster was clearly suspicious of Ardell's casual attitude to his impending death. "What is your request?"

"I'd like to see Heinrich Müller before you shoot me."

Oster glared. "You mean the head of the Gestapo? *That* Heinrich Müller?"

Ardell smiled amiably. "The very same."

Tall Square leaned close to Oster. Over the not-so-distant sounds of battle Ardell could just make out his words, "He's up to something, sir. I say we just shoot him and be done with it."

Oster seemed to wrestle with himself. Ardell could just imagine his Teutonic quandary of expediency versus protocol versus basic human curiosity.

Apparently the last one won. *Or else whatever happens he's decided he can blame it on Müller.* "What do you need to see him for?"

"To make my last report."

"Your last—"

Tall Square shook his head emphatically. "I don't like it, sir. If he's Gestapo—"

Oster seemed resigned. "Can we get Müller down here?"

Tall Square seemed to deflate. "Probably?"

Oster gave Short Round a look, and the other man shouldered his rifle and trotted off.

Tall Square gave Oster a look of his own, but by now the Master-At-Arms was deliberately not paying him any attention.

Ardell took a long drag and exhaled with forced indifference.

"Hey, Big Guy... you think I could get another cigarette when this one's gone?"

They made him stand outside in the rain while Müller was summoned. Oster took Galya to a nearby hole in the wall where they could shelter from the rain while he explained to her how to fill out the paperwork. She glanced up to Ardell only once with a question in her blue eyes, but he gave her one quick shake of the head and looked away.

After about a half hour there was the sound of a car engine entering the gate to Ardell's distant left and about another ten minutes later Müller himself, scowling and covering his head with a manila folder, emerged into the garden. "What is it you need that is so important, Oster?"

Oster's demeanor was superficially deferential, but Ardell could tell by his stance he was just as put out by this development as Müller. "Herr Müller. Thank you for coming. This man was asking for you."

Müller turned to look and started. "Klugmann!" he exclaimed with genuine surprise. "What on earth are you doing here?"

"Hello, sir," Ardell offered innocently.

Müller turned back to Oster. "What on earth is he doing here? Why is he up against that wall?"

Oster's tone became defensive. "His papers were falsified, sir. See for yourself." He pushed Ardell's papers into the Gestapo chief's hands.

Müller gave them a perfunctory once-over and his brows knit together in puzzlement.

"Thirty-Second Grenadiers? Kobus, what is the meaning of this? Where did you get these papers?"

"I made them myself, sir."

"Kobus, Kobus, you aren't a forger! Doing things like this can get you into serious trouble!"

Oster rocked back on his heels and crossed his arms. "Then he *is* one of yours, Herr Müller?"

Müller sighed. "You can let him go, Oster. I will get to the bottom of this. Kobus!"

"Sir?"

"See me in the Gestapo office on the second floor right away. But get out of that uniform first." He looked askance at Oster and his goons. "It doesn't suit you."

VII

THE RAIN continued into the next morning. The dismal weather, together with the low clouds, smoldering fires and billows of smoke combined to create an aura worthy of Dante's First Circle of Hell. Even the shapeless civilians furtively dashing through the ruins evoked feelings of the Unrighteous struggling to avoid the arrows of centaurs and the judging tail of Minos.

Ardell thought it ironic that it was the literary image of the Gateway that was echoed outside the gaping holes in the Chancellery walls where windows used to be. He may not have been able to see the battlefront from the Chancellery yet, but he could easily imagine what was coming for the city, and Dante hadn't been even half right.

Today he was wearing an ill-fitting civilian suit as Müller's had requested when he entered the RSD office looking for Galya. He still needed to get out of the city and, according to what he had overheard the day before, just slipping out on his own was not going to be an option.

He found her at the counter, frowning as she sorted through files. The inebriate Lily was notably absent.

"Good morning!" Ardell began with forced cheerfulness.

Galya looked up. "Why hello!" She did a double take at his frumpy attire. "Looks like you took care of things with Müller?"

"Old buddies again." Ardell confirmed.

"Old buddies... again? So that explains his reaction yesterday." She knit her delicate brows together and dropped her voice to a whisper. "But I thought you were OSS? Or FBI, weren't you? Or is it both? Are you still?"

"Was, are, both... my girl, there's more to me than—"

"—than meets the eye."

Ardell nodded and smiled approvingly. English idioms had been one of Galya's fascinations for as long as he'd known her.

She returned the smile with some appreciation. "So it seems. And now we can add Gestapo to that list. You're a double agent." She cast her eyes to the ceiling in contemplation and curled her finger over her chin. "Or triple, if you're counting." Her voice took on a more conversational tone. "So how long have you been on a Deutschmark payroll? You weren't Gestapo in Dresden."

"How do you know I wasn't?"

"Because I do my homework, my love."

"Fair enough. Not quite a year now."

She nodded, eyes calculating. "And for a year's seniority, what does Müller have you up to now?"

"Well, since we've we patched things up, he likes me so much he has me setting up his office upstairs."

"I have a feeling," Galya offered impishly, "that when he got back to the RSHA building last evening things weren't quite as he was expecting."

Ardell nodded. "Apparently the Reds were already breaking into the west end and he had to grab what he could and make a hasty exit the other way." He had to admit her intel was remarkably up to date. That at least was reassuring. Nevertheless, Ardell felt this was a good time to change focus. He still needed to feel out Galya's position before he asked her what he had come for. "What about you? What are you cataloging so diligently?"

"Background checks for Knight's Cross candidates. Make sure their bloodlines are satisfactory, their politics are in line, that sort of thing."

"Because when the Nazis win the war, we have to make sure all the awards can be properly handed out."

"That's right, Kobus, my love." She regarded him closely, but Ardell was too good an agent to let something slip *that* easily.

Her expression became serious as she turned back to her papers. "So. Are you going to turn me in?"

"No. You don't have to worry about that."

She glanced at him sideways and smiled. "I don't? Is that because you love me so much?"

Ardell shook his head. "It's because I can't afford any distractions."

"Ahh.... Company man, are you? Is it that big a mission?"

There was a loud explosion a few blocks away that echoed through the broken windows and Ardell started. "Damn! That was close!"

Galya lifted her chin as if she were sniffing the air. "Tiger tank."

"That was no eighty-eight."

"Not the gun, Kobus. It was the tank going up." She crinkled her nose. "Russians, you know."

"You can tell by the sound?"

"Since Rostov? Yes, I can tell." She fiddled around with the papers some more. "Must have complicated your mission, having to put yourself under Müller's nose like you did. Now you're stuck doing his scut work." She dropped a thick sheaf behind a filing cabinet with a miffed flourish. "You should have let me draw up your papers, darling."

"I do seem to recall that being a knack of yours." He watched her bend over to pull another stack of papers out of a box on the floor. "Among other things... hmm..."

Galya stood and turned, catching him staring. "What?"

"Real nylons!" He pointed at her calves. "Not just a line drawn up the back of your—"

She slapped him with a manila folder. "I hear the Reds are less than a half-kilometer away."

"Yes, well..." Ardell took the hint, and decided it was time to use the opening. "About that... I need a favor."

Galya slid shut the drawer she was working on and turned fully toward him. "Oh, really?"

"Don't get so excited... Okay, you can get excited..." He took a deep breath. He *really* hated having to ask for help. "I need to get out of the city."

"Your mission is over already?"

"Mission's been scrubbed."

"Has it? Why? You just got here."

Ardell fidgeted.

"Delly?" Her voice was not nearly as endearing as the use of the pet name suggested. "Why?"

Damn! "My father is here."

"Your—" For once he could tell he had caught her completely off guard. *Glad I'm not the only one,* he thought bitterly.

His next thought was no more palatable. *I'm going to have to tell her, just for the sake of disclosure.* "He's one of the tank commanders. I ran into him in the officer's mess last night."

"The he saw you?"

"Oh, yes."

"And recognized you."

"Oh... yes."

She nodded to herself. "You don't think he would cover for you?"

He thought back to that day, ten years ago, when he and Mom had left. "I honestly don't think he's physically capable of lying."

"But would he just keep quiet, for your sake?"

"I don't know." Memories crowded his mind, recollections of bitter words hurled in anger. "We didn't part on the best of terms."

"I see." She folded her arms and cocked her head at him. "And your boys didn't plan you an extraction?"

"Don't get me started. But *your* boys, like you said, are only a half-kilometer away."

She nodded again, half to herself, and slowly her contemplative frown turned into a delighted smile. "Ah! *You* need *me* to get *you* out!" She folded her arms, rocked back on one hip and licked her teeth. "The great Ardell Murto, legend among the cloak-and-dagger gang, needs *my* help!"

"You don't have to sound so thrilled about it."

"Oh, but I am! I am!" She threw her arms in the air and draped them over his neck. "Because as it turns out, I need help from *you*." She pulled him in close and whispered in his ear. "Maybe we can work out an arrangement?"

Ardell gently reached up and pulled her arms back down by the wrists. "What help do you need?"

Galya pouted. "Don't get cocky, Kobus, my love. Beggars can't be choosers, you know."

"Quit using my own idioms against me." His tone was annoyed but the grimace on his face revealed his resignation to being backed into a corner. "But you're right. I'm begging. Okay, so how can I help?" he finished with a smile that would befit a ten-year-old asking what chores they can do for a slice of cake.

She pulled him out into the hallway where the ambient noise was louder and overhearing ears were more distant. "I need you to get me in close to the target."

"What target?" Ardell countered.

"Come on, Ardell, we both know you're here for the same reason as I."

"Maybe so. Though for significantly different reasons."

"Whatever. Ultimately, we want the same thing. You can't get what you want for why you want it, so you may as well help me get what I want for why I want it."

Ardell growled under his breath, which only elicited a coy smile from Galya. "Fine! And what exactly am I doing?"

"Why, using your cover, darling. I'm just a low-level stenographer. But you..." she plucked at his suit and tidied his tie. "You are a Gestapo agent and the current favorite of their director!"

Ardell sighed and nodded. "Okay. I can make that work. How soon?"

"Now that's the trick for *you*, Delly. I need you to sit tight until *I* tell you it's time to move."

"Yeah... this is why I always liked to work the solo missions."

"I know, love. Oh, do I know. *I* remember Dresden!"

"So do I."

Galya squealed and clapped her hands. "Oh, this is absolutely delicious. Kobus, I am so glad you came to me!"

"Why do I feel this is going to end up as a really lopsided deal?"

Galya frowned at the unfamiliar word. Ardell rolled his eyes. "Okay. Try 'one-sided'?"

Her expression brightened. "Ah! I can see your concerns. You don't like it because you're not in control."

"That's not it."

"You know, for an operative you are a terrible liar." She wagged a finger at him. "Are you getting what you want?"

"In a sense."

She held up a second finger. "Are you getting out?"

"So I've been told."

Galya pouted again and curled her fingers back into a fist. "Kobus! Why are you so brutal with my feelings?"

"You know there's no room for feelings in this line of work."

"Exactly!" she pounced. "You just swallow that oversized pride, my love, and trust me that I care about you enough to keep my end of the bargain!"

"'Care enough'? No offense, and thanks in advance, but... you care about me? Why? May I ask?" He realized it sounded more accusatory than he intended and tried to mitigate the harsh tone with a softer finish.

Galya's face likewise went soft, almost sentimental. "Because, Ardell Murto, you saved my life in Dresden. Though you didn't know it." She reached up and patted him on the chest. "I feel I owe you. And you're welcome."

Ardell hung his head sheepishly. "Fine. I'll take your word for it. So... any idea when it *will* be time to move?"

She shook her head. "Not yet. I'm still... how do you say? Dancing to a... no, that's not it. Help me out, Kobus!"

"Playing it by ear?"

She smiled, a genuine expression this time. "Yes!" She turned back toward the RSD office door. "Don't worry, Delly. I have you under my wing now. When it *is* time, where will I find you?"

Ardell jerked his chin upward. "Second floor, street side of this wing facing the parking garage. Müller wanted to be able to see the Reichtag."

"He's going to be disappointed. Is the office marked?" She tapped the letters painted on her door.

"Not yet. But you won't be able to miss it. Just look for a couple big boys in black uniforms and blank stares."

"Sounds definitive. What are we doing about your father?"

Ardell huffed out a breath and looked in the general direction of the sounds of battle. "Well, if I'm going to be serving your highness' pleasure, I'm going to have to talk to him and see if I can buy a little more time. Like you said, all he needs to do is not say anything."

"You'll have to keep a close eye on him, I'm afraid."

"Well, you know what they say... 'Keep your friends close, and your enemies closer.'"

Galya stepped back up to him and pecked him on the cheek. "And family closest of all?"

In the barracks the men were preparing for action. Some were eager, most were wary, all were tired, and everywhere gear was spread out in small piles, getting cleaned, organized, packed and loaded under the unforgiving eye of company quartermasters.

Rolf stepped carefully between each man's impromptu domain and took stock of how things looked as he went. He tried to offer words of encouragement or reassurance where he thought to, but the looks he got from his men in return varied from sullen skepticism to outright cynical disbelief. Speaking such empty platitudes to those going into the breach like this had always made him self-conscious. He was sure his men could tell he didn't believe the words himself and worried that they resented his efforts for thinking they would. It wasn't that he didn't care about them—he did, incredibly acutely so, but he was ever at a loss to make that apparent. *Fournier is so much better at this,* he thought, and consoled himself with the idea that the Frenchman would be making his own rounds through the men soon enough to smooth things over.

He passed out into the street where his vehicles were parked in the rubble of an adjacent building under cover and reached into his pocket to feel the reassuring plastic form of Dieter's toy soldier. He hadn't slept well the night before. The shock of seeing Ardell, here, in Berlin of all places, and in a German uniform, had put him into a deep funk, and even what he had learned during a handful of sessions with Herr Asperger in Vienna were insufficient to help him make a place in his thoughts for how he felt. It was apparent enough what his son was doing in the city. He didn't need his background as a mathematician to figure *that* out.

Against his will he found his thoughts plunging headlong into the past. He had tried to communicate with Margaret for a time after their split, he honestly had, as far as he could tell. But his letters had gone unanswered and transatlantic phone calls were expensive and difficult just for technical reasons alone. Never mind the bitterness thrown at him when he finally was able to make a connection. And Ardell... the boy never would speak on the phone and there was no doubt Margaret had used her chance at his undivided attention to fill his son's head with an image of an ardent Nazi that chose Party over family.

He hadn't, in his mind. He had been stuck 'between two chairs', as his own mother had used to say, forced to choose between an all-powerful government on one side and an inflexible wife on the other. And in the end, it was Margaret who had made the choice of ideology over family.

But while his letters were never answered, every so often he *would* get something—usually an offhand announcement of some kind, like an invitation to see Ardell receiving some award in school. Invariably it would be postmarked mere days before the event so as to be sure to arrive too late, and would be followed by a small photo weeks later of the two of them smiling and embracing at the ceremony, as if to twist the knife just that much more. This was how Rolf had learned that Ardell had joined the police academy, and his entry into the FBI. It was a short leap from there to guess his son's move to the OSS and his presence here now.

Still, he was worried. As if it wasn't bad enough thinking about how he was going to get his men out of this ever-tightening Red noose, now he had to worry about his oldest son.

Whether or not that son believed he cared.

He rounded the fender of the radio track and poked his head in the side door.

"All set, Eemi?"

Eemi leaned back in his seat and cast his eyes across his radio gear. He blew out a breath and slammed his fist against one of the sets. "I don't have the tubes to make the Eleven unit work."

Rolf frowned sympathetically. "I don't think we're going to need the long-range radios, Eemi." He didn't mean for it to sound condescending but the look on Eemi's face said it all. "How is the Twelve?" he quickly added.

Eemi flipped a few switches and paused as the unit warmed up. "Seems to be good, sir."

"Good. You have your gear ready?"

Eemi slapped a rucksack stashed under the radio mounts and nodded.

"Right... Eemi?"

Eemi paused and turned around with that perplexed expression Rolf so often got from other people whenever he tried to tell them something he felt was important. Margaret had told him once it was because other people could never figure out from his expressions and tone what his intentions were. For his part, Rolf had always figured the words themselves would make their gravity apparent. "Sir?" the young man asked with raised eyebrows.

"I heard one of Krebs' aides was able to make it out of the city to the west last night," he began. "He headed out to the U-bahn at the Zoo and was able to pass under the Russian lines to the Stadium."

"He was lucky, sounds like. The Reds are all over the Zoo now, sir."

Rolf nodded. "Yes. You'd probably have to enter the U-bahn at Kaiserhof and double back from there."

Now Eemi looked genuinely puzzled. "*I* would, sir? Are you sending me out?"

Rolf realized that he hadn't fully told Eemi what he had been thinking before he had started speaking. "No, not specifically. But I want you to consider it. If things get too heavy here—"

"But sir!" Eemi seemed genuinely shocked. "I can't just... what about everyone else?"

His reaction surprised Rolf, who had thoroughly worked out the logic of his advice early this morning. "Eemi, listen... you're young, you have family west of the Elbe, including a young wife, and don't you have a baby?" It made no sense for the boy to throw all that away on this fool's errand of defending the city to the end.

"Well, yes, sir, but I... what of the rest of the men? What about the people? I mean, why me? There are other guys that could—"

"—And I intend to speak to them as well. Eemi... look, I just want you to consider it. Not as your commanding officer, but as..." He hesitated to say *as a friend;* he had never thought of himself as such to the troops in his charge, but he *had* always thought of himself in the role of protector and advocate. "... As just a wise thing to do."

Eemi frowned as if he had been insulted. He even seemed hurt. "Okay, sir... I will consider it." He slowly put his headphones back on, his face deep in worry.

"Good." Rolf breathed deep, glad the exchange was over and the idea was out there. He ducked back out of the hatch and stood to see Ardell approaching from the head of the line. He was wearing a suit adorned with a Gestapo badge on the breast.

Rolf drew a deep breath and exhaled slowly. Dealing with tactical situations, ranges and angles of fire, fuel and ammunition supplies... these were easy for him. Dealing with his men and their myriad personalities he often left to others. But addressing whatever his own son was about to bring to him was not something he could math out or delegate away, and the thought caused his chest to draw up tight like a cinch.

There was a natural part of him that wanted to keep Ardell close, to find a way to get him out of the city. *Why here, now, of all places and times?* he thought bitterly.

But then the inevitable 'what-ifs' and 'what-abouts' started. *Shouldn't he already have a way out? Surely his superiors provided for one. What if he doesn't want my help? He made it pretty clear that I was to stay away.*

What if he didn't need a way out? What if he wasn't expected to get out? What if... He crushed that thought before it could take any further form. There was nothing good to be found going down *that* path.

He assumed a casual stance with his hands in his pockets, partly to answer the ever-present question of what to do with them as much as to allow him to grip Dieter's toy soldier for the spare comfort it afforded.

Ardell approached with a deliberate step though he at least had the sense to stay close to the broken walls around him for cover. He stopped just out of arm's reach.

"Can we talk for a minute?"

That was it, no niceties, no familiarity. Rolf knew in his mind that his son's role here as a spy was the biggest reason for this, but his heart still sank at the tone of the words.

"Sure. I have a moment. What... what can I help you with, Officer?"

Ardell looked around, stepped up close and spoke in low tones. "I've scrubbed my mission. But I need some time to leave the city. Maybe some hours, maybe some days. What do you want in exchange for not saying anything to anyone about me?"

"Exchange?" Rolf was stung that Ardell thought his protection was something that needed bargaining for. He felt the cinch around his chest drop into his gut.

"Yes, exchange. What do you want me to do for you?" Ardell hadn't seemed to notice the ache in Rolf's voice or what it meant, but he did notice the bulk of his father's fist in his pocket and was apparently able to deduce why that was. "You want me to get Dieter out safely, right? You don't want to leave him here in all this chaos?"

As if the weight on his chest wasn't enough, now Rolf was thunderstruck. Why on earth would anyone, let alone his own flesh and blood, think he would have brought Dieter into all this? "Dieter's not here, so—Officer."

Ardell's eyes never flickered. "Oh. I see. So you left him behind somewhere. That sounds familiar."

"Now wait a minute!" Rolf's deference to Ardell's cover took a sudden back seat to his anger. "Wait just a minute! You don't get to sneer at me about having your brother here and then criticize me for not!"

Ardell made a hasty shushing gesture with his hands and Rolf grudgingly bit his tongue. He dropped his voice and whispered through clenched teeth. "Dieter is in *Arpke* with his *aunt*. I sent him there because I knew the Americans would get there *first* and he would be safer with *them*. And for the *record...*" He fought down the growl that was creeping into his voice, "it was you that chose to leave, not me."

Ardell frowned and exhaled sharply through his nose. "I know. Not you. You were just doing what you were told. It was easier that way for you, wasn't it?"

"Easier? You think this—" he waved a hand at the shattered city, "—was *easier?*"

"It's what you chose to do, wasn't it?"

"What would you have had me do? Lie to them? You know what that would have led to!"

"What I *wanted* you to do was come with us. But you couldn't. Or *wouldn't.*"

Rolf knew his anger and frustration was blatant on his face, but he couldn't form an answer to Ardell's last barb. There had been so many reasons, for and against on each side of that argument, and he had been paralyzed trying to choose. Paralyzed until the choice had been made for him then, and just as frozen now, dumping them all out fresh in his mind like a tipped-over trash can.

But it was clear Ardell took his silence for a concession. "Yeah. Like I thought. You just were not going to give me what I needed."

At that Rolf found his tongue. "Wrong, Ardell. I gave you what you *needed*. A home. Food on the table. Clothes on your back when everyone else was begging in the streets. An education." He scoffed and gestured at Ardell's badge. "A respect for duty. A sense of right and wrong. That's right!" he snapped at the surprise on Ardell's face. "Even if you're using it against me, I at least taught you how to make up your own mind!" He crossed his arms so Ardell couldn't see his fists and turned his face away. "That was what I was supposed to give you as your father. What I couldn't give you, it seems, is what you *wanted*. There's a difference, and you need to know it."

"Why?" Ardell's voice was caustic. "Why does it make a difference? What I 'want', what I 'need'?"

"Because I felt the same about my father! And I'm sure he felt the same about his! And you," he turned to face his son fully once more, "if fortune smiles for *you*, one day when you're out of this place you will have a son of your own. And you will do everything you can for him, but you will still find there are things *he* wants that you're not going to be able to give him!"

"Yeah? Like what? Seems all I need to do, is not be like you!"

"How about respect for anyone's feelings but your own?"

Rolf clenched his teeth and his fists, squeezing the toy soldier so hard the edges bit into his palm. He realized he was panting and he forced himself to slow his breathing.

They stared daggers at each other for several more heartbeats until a lone Focke-Wulf screamed overhead at low level followed by a finger-four of Russian Yaks. Tracer fire slid past the German machine which failed to jink out of the way and began trailing smoke. The chase then disappeared beyond the rooftops as quickly as it had arrived, except for one Russian plane that circled back to open fire on a large communication balloon tethered over the Chancellery. There was a quick flash of flame as the rounds found their target and the balloon fell, dropping the attached radio-telephone antenna to the ground.

Rolf straightened up and drew another deep breath. He let it out in a slow, even measure, but his eyes were afire. "How about this, *Officer*? Do you want to know what I want? Instead of you telling me what you 'know' I want?"

Ardell chewed his lip for a moment before answering a surly, "Sure."

Rolf looked at the halftrack behind him as if he could see through the armor plating to the young radioman inside. "You've seen the death squads on the way in, haven't you? You must have."

Ardell nodded, once.

"I want you to do something about that. I want you to use that—" he pointed at the badge on Ardell's coat, "and do something about it. *That* is my condition. You do that and I won't tell anyone that you're my son." He turned half away toward the next vehicle in line, then stopped and looked back over his shoulder.

"Or at least that you were, once upon a time."

VIII

B Y MID-AFTERNOON Ardell had managed to pull enough strings to set things in motion.

He stood in the doorway of Müller's office. For the moment he was alone. He stepped toward the window in the western wall, careful to stay well back and to one side in case there were any snipers along the southern edge of the Tiergarten. If he looked out at just the right angle with his binoculars, he could see down the Potsdammerstraße where a clutch of civilians moved in a loose square. *Volkssturm,* Ardell decided. They suddenly stopped, like a wave breaking on shore, when a Soviet column of infantry and lightly-built T-70's appeared around a corner some blocks away. There were trails of smoke from the Germans as panzerfausts were fired, and the lead Russian tank went up in a rather anti-climactic bluff of smoke and rolled to a stop.

A heavier T-34 shoved the stricken vehicle out of the way and fired into the Volkssturm with what Ardell assumed was a high-explosive round, given the pink-tinged blast that resulted. When the smoke cleared the Volkssturm were gone and the Russians were charging ahead.

There was another trail of fire from an empty-eyed apartment building and the T-34's engine burst into flames. The crew bailed out to join their supposedly protective infantry but this proved fatal as an MG 42 opened up from an upper-floor balcony. The Reds dove for cover and Ardell watched with a spectator's detachment as a handful breached the streetside door and poured in.

Some minutes later there were a series of flashes inside the upper floors, and bodies began dropping out the windows.

The sound of a door opening to his left caught his attention and he lowered the binoculars. Galya entered, steno pad in hand, and held the door for Fengeler who did a double take at Ardell's presence in civilian clothes.

Ardell nodded a bland acknowledgment and moved to the southern edge of the window to look toward the Reichtag. As Galya had predicted, the view was poor, not so much due to the city's layout as much as the smoke overlaying everything. Planes were cruising overhead, but Ardell was sure any desire on the part of their pilots to find targets of opportunity were being frustrated by the horrible visibility.

There was a thick-sounding 'fump' on the desk to his left and he turned to see Müller had arrived and dropped a heavy file on his desk. Ardell drew himself up to attention, as did Fengeler, but the latter snapped to much more ardently, as if he were trying to show Ardell how it was done.

Müller sat and motioned everyone else to do likewise.

Fengeler remained standing. "Is this going to take long, Herr Müller?"

Müller frowned. "Do you have somewhere else to be, Colonel?"

Fengeler pointed with his service cap out the window that was vibrating to the sound of the ever-creeping artillery fire. "I am tasked with seeing that cowards and deserters are brought back to the fight. So, yes, I *do*, in fact, have somewhere to be, Herr Chief."

Müller was decidedly nonplussed. "Yes, about that. For the record," he glanced at Galya, who was scribbling in rapid shorthand, "state your full name, please?"

"Is this a formal inquisition?"

"I am asking the questions, Herr Colonel."

"So you are..." Fengeler sat abruptly and crossed his legs. "Very well. I am Colonel Helmut Olbright Fengeler, Waffen-SS."

"Yes... let's see what I've found here." Müller opened the file, flipped through a few pages, and began reading. "Doctorate of Anthropology from the University of Marburg,

Class of Twenty-Nine." He skipped down to the bottom of the page. "Associate Professor of Religious Culture... you were part of the Tibetan Expedition in Thirty-Eight?"

Fengeler's chin lifted even more than usual. "I documented racial archetypes for the Ancestral Heritage Society."

"That must have been fascinating." Müller's tone was as dry as an Egyptian pharaoh.

His sarcasm, though, seemed lost on Fengeler. "It was, actually. I saw impressive temples, stunning palaces, beautiful tombs... marvels of civic industry. But the depravity carved on their walls..." He shook his head and barreled on, oblivious to Müller's attempt to start speaking again. "Structures built by great races in the distant past whose degenerate descendants are now little more than brutes pissing on their own floors."

"The expedition," Müller interjected as Fengeler stopped to draw breath. "This is how you came to be in the SS?"

"It was a condition of Herr Himmler's sponsorship."

"But you were not *Waffen*-SS." The Gestapo Chief flipped more pages. "That came later, in 1941."

Fengeler's voice grew icy. "Let's just say I saw things on the way home that inspired the change."

Müller eyed Fengeler closely. "Indeed." He paged further back into the record. "By the opening of Operation Barbarossa, you were in the *Einsatzgruppen*."

"I had come to realize I was better suited to more... direct action."

"Hence your current assignment."

"From which this proceeding is keeping me."

Müller frowned again and slapped the dossier closed. "Herr Klugmann, why don't you relate what you told me earlier? And perhaps," he glanced around to Fengeler, "you can add some background to give our guest a little context."

Fengeler tossed his cap impatiently on the desk.

Ardell took a deep breath. "Of course, sir." *Showtime.* "For some time now, I have been working as a double agent." He stood and forced himself to pace in a relaxed manner. "Herr Müller had seconded me to the SD so I could take up a position in the Allied High Command."

"That was about a year ago," Müller added.

Ardell nodded and continued, "While I was in London, I found that the Allies were getting very accurate information about what was happening on the Eastern Front, in particular the sectors controlled by the SS. This information was better than what they were getting from the Reds themselves."

Fengeler looked skeptical, so Ardell explained. "There seems to be an inordinate level of rivalry, and even mistrust, between Comrade Stalin and the other Allied leadership. In any case, I allowed myself to be recruited into the OSS and managed to get myself sent to infiltrate Luftflotte Four Command, where I was closer to the front and could carry out my own investigation. As the Soviets advanced on our capital the information flow continued and became even more specific. This eventually led me to make my way back into the city, which I effected yesterday—"

Across the street the rubble next to Rolf's barracks was hit by an artillery salvo and everyone flinched reflexively.

"With all due respect, Herr Müller," Fengeler snarled, "Get to the point, Klugmann!"

"Yes. Yes! The short version, sirs, is simply this: *Someone* has been sending soldiers out of the city, supposedly to link up with intact units beyond the Russian forces. But these men are not carrying out these missions. They are simply deserting to the west, and they are the ones providing the Allies this information."

There was dead silence in the room for several seconds. Even the guns outside seemed to hold their fire long enough for the implication of Ardell's statement to sink in. Müller sat, staring directly at Fengeler, whose face quickly went from bored disinterest to outright indignation.

"Are you accusing my men—"

"I am." Müller's voice was as flat and heavy as a concrete bunker.

"That's preposterous!"

"Is it, Herr Colonel? Can you account for all your teams?"

"The city is swarming with Russian barbarians! Men go out and don't return. It is what happens!"

"Can you prove Herr Klugmann wrong?" Müller charged.

"Can you prove him *right?* This is outrageous!" He stood and snatched his cap off Müller's desk and shook it at the Gestapo Chief, punctuating his ire with it. "You obstruct my obligation to the Reich with trivialities!"

Müller was no less offended. "Calm down, Herr Colonel. This is very important—"

"Important to the *Gestapo.*" Fengeler's voice dripped with distaste. "As you two sit in this office, while my men fight and die in the streets!"

Fengeler drew himself up and thrust his chin into the air. "*We* are Waffen-SS. *We* are not afraid to take the fight right to the enemy face-to-face. *We* do not skulk about in plain coats and batter down the doors of widows in the night! Herr Klugmann!"

Ardell was caught momentarily off guard as the shorter man turned on him. "Sir?"

"Do you have any actual evidence against me?"

Ardell assumed a mellow demeanor. "I do not, actually, Herr Colonel. Nothing definitive."

"Then, Herr Müller, with your leave—or without, in fact—I have duties to which I must attend." He turned and marched out, straight as a ramrod.

There was another awkward silence, but this time the guns outside had resumed. Ardell waited and Galya sat, pencil poised, both of them watching Müller stonily regard the door.

After a moment Müller grunted and hefted the file folder on his desk. "I have heard enough. I will take this up with General Weidling. Miss Heffenbach, I need you to draft me a request to put a stop to Fengeler's courts martial in the Citadel Sector effective immediately. Herr Klugmann, you are dismissed."

Galya stepped quickly to catch up with Ardell as he left the office. She slipped her hand through the crook of his elbow but her grip on his bicep was anything but friendly.

"I thought I told you to lay low!" she hissed.

"You said nothing of the sort," Ardell countered, offended. "You said to sit tight."

"It's the same thing, Delly."

"Hardly. 'Sit tight' means to bide one's time—"

"Exactly. To stay out of the way." Her voice took on a lecturing tone. "First used by Sir Robert Baden-Powell in his 1896 book *The Matabele Campaign.* 'They would sit tight and strike out hard.'"

"Right. The Matabele would wait for the opportune moment and then attack the Brits. The implication is definitely not that they were sitting around doing nothing. You know, I may be a terrible liar, as you claim, but at least I don't get my metaphors mixed up. I thought you made a study of English?"

The scandalized look on her face was almost worth the price of admission.

"And you're not even using the one you *are* using, correctly," he continued. "You don't want me to 'lay low'. That's what you do to someone when you defeat them, like a boxer lays his opponent low with a knockout. You actually want me to 'lie low', as in cower, hide... like in a foxhole." He waved a hand at the now constant rumble of artillery fire to add emphasis.

Galya finally managed to find her voice. "Yes, dammit! Whatever! The point is you were supposed to stay out of sight! What's with stirring the pot—*am I using that one correctly, Delly?*—with Fengeler? It's not like the Reds aren't going to deal with him soon enough in any case!"

"This may surprise you, my love, but I actually *am* trying to stay out of sight."

"Oh? I can't wait for you to explain this one."

"You remember my father knows I'm here? And I had to buy more time for you? So I did... and this was the payment."

"To take out Fengeler?"

"Basically. To stop his death squads."

"You got the only other person who knows who you are to keep quiet by going after what is probably one of the highest profile targets in the Chancellery."

"Don't lecture me about high-profile targets, dear."

"Sounds like he's setting you up for failure.... How much do you trust him?"

That stopped Ardell in his tracks and for a moment he fumbled for a response. "You know... I have to admit I hadn't thought of it that way. But now that you mention it... I *did* think it was uncharacteristically altruistic of him."

Now it was Galya's turn to be puzzled. "Okay, Delly. I have to know. In the interest of disclosure. What exactly happened between you two?"

"I'm afraid you're going to just have to trust me when I say it's not actually relevant."

"You know I can't allow anything—"

"—that will compromise your mission," Ardell finished. "I know. I do this for a living, too, you know." He turned fully toward her and held her by the shoulders. "Trust me. It isn't relevant."

"You're not going to tell me? At all?"

"There's no time to explain it all. But don't worry. If it was going to be a problem, I would sit you down and run you through the whole thing,"

Galya cocked her head to one side and pursed her lips. "You shouldn't always playthings so close to the vest..." Her eyebrows rose with the question and Ardell smirked at her correct use of the idiom.

She gave him a half-annoyed shove. "You always think you can control the situation."

"It's how I stay alive, my love."

"Well... one day you're going to see that some things will be beyond your control no matter what you do. Speaking of which..." She thoughtfully poked her tongue out one side of her mouth, "you're supposed to be keeping your family close. Where is your tank commander now? Don't you need to let him know you've kept your end of the bargain?"

Ardell's eyes went wide. "Damn! You're right. I've got to get to the barracks." He leaned down and pecked her on the cheek. "See you later, dear. Stay out of the sniper sights while I'm gone!"

It was harder getting across the street this time. He made the mistake of stepping out the west exit door without looking and was rewarded with a bullet taking out a chink of masonry by his head. He ducked back in, circled around the SS barracks to the northwest corner of the complex, and was a lot more careful scurrying across the open street on his second attempt.

It was all for naught, though. When he got to the apartment block the rooms were empty but for the occasional dropped ration can or letter from home, and the ringing echoes of war coming from the Tiergarten.

In its heyday the Tiergarten had been one of the largest urban parks in Europe. Frederick the Great had taken what had until then been the private hunting grounds of the Prussian kings and opened them to the public and had it fully decked out in full Baroque splendor. Flowerbeds punctuated by hedge mazes and ornamental ponds dotted with more bridges than anyone could reliably count had been sheltered under tens of thousands of stately linden trees.

Now, though, the Animal Park was a mere nightmarish shadow of its former self. Trees which would have been barren awaiting the arrival of spring had been blasted before they could leaf by Allied bombing raids and Soviet artillery. Ponds were replaced by shell craters which, with the loss of Templehof, had been filled in on the western end of Charlottenburger Chaussee to allow pilots brave enough to risk it a dangerous and limited aerial route in and out of the city.

Now the sky was still a depressing low-slung gray, adding a forlorn counterpoint to the devastation on the ground. Rolf stood on the southern edge of the grounds where the Hofjägerallee passed out of the park and surveyed the Russian movements across the Landwehr canal. Behind him the rumble of Maybach engines marked the burning of precious fuel as his Tigers moved into position while immediately before him only empty pedestals remained where proud Berliners had removed elegant statues to safer havens. Rolf knew those responsible were fearful of losing what heritage they had left from before the Nazi dominion, and he couldn't blame them, but he marveled that they had become so numb to the dangers that they had been willing to risk the crossfire to actually accomplish it.

He had placed sharpshooters in the buildings on his southern flank and they were keeping themselves busy preventing the Reds from bringing up field guns from Charlottenburg. Nevertheless, every Soviet that fell to their guns provided a little bit more cover to the rest coming up behind them, and despite the carnage the swarming Easterners were managing to float pontoon bridges across the canal.

Rolf watched the bridgeheads creep closer, hull by hull. Behind them katyusha launchers were taking their places among the shattered buildings while brigades of infantry flowed through it all like scum on a pond. "Fournier!" he called with an edge in his voice.

"Sir?"

"How are your preparations going?"

"Better, sir. General Krukenberg was able to find us some ammo and about a hundred police officers."

"Finally. Where are you placing the men?"

"Haven't worked that out yet, sir, they've only just arrived."

Rolf eyed the buildings housing his sharpshooters. "Put them in there on the lower floors. They can watch the backs of our lads up top."

"Right, sir."

Rolf shook his head again. *Old men and boys. What have we come to?* He looked to the southwest toward the Zoo where a massive monolith loomed over the smoke of a hundred fires. Every few seconds a flash illuminated its flanks as the Soviets threw shells at it with no effect. "Are we in communication with the flak tower?"

"We are. They're loaded and ready to go."

Rolf pointed back across the canal. "The Reds are still hiding among the buildings. We need to get them to overextend, draw them out into the open where the flak tower can hit them."

"Any idea how to do that?"

"Yes. But you're not going to like it."

"After all this I don't like any of it. What could be worse?"

"Good point." Rolf hiked a thumb over his shoulder. "Tell the crews not to bother digging in. Get them up on that rise over there, more in the open."

Fournier looked apprehensive. "But they'll see we only have a few panzers left."

"Right. It will make them overconfident. They will strike before they are ready. Besides, we need the mobility. Do we have a fallback position?"

"Yes, two hundred meters northeast. Though there's not much left beyond that."

"That will have to do. Make it happen, Fournier, and tell the men once we're out to just be ready to keep going."

"Right." He paused for a heartbeat, watching Rolf expectantly. When Rolf didn't notice, Fournier nodded to himself and cleared his throat. "Um, Captain? A question..."

"Yes?"

"You said to be ready to keep going. May I ask where?"

"Does it matter at this point?"

"Well, we've been talking of breaking out to the north, but I'm not sure we will get the tracks across the Spree—"

"There will be no breakout to the north. Not to the north, or anywhere else."

Fournier bit back whatever he was about to say and nodded his understanding. "Right. I'll tell the men." He turned and started up the line, shouting loudly. Rolf couldn't tell if it was out of anger, frustration, or fear.

The Reds were finally settled in enough to start firing volleys of rockets. These came in heavy hissing flocks, not like their normal handful as they tried to find the range. Rolf knew they were firing blind, that they hadn't actually spotted his tracks, and were just softening up the park and hoping to keep the heads of any would-be snipers down while they finished their bridgehead.

Unfortunately for them Rolf's Hitlerjugende were no longer afraid of the blasts and were letting the Soviets have it back in spades. A part of Rolf was proud of them for overcoming their combat jitters, but a bigger part was heartsick that such a thing was even necessary at their age.

Old men and boys.... He clenched the toy soldier in his pocket and looked wistfully northward.

There was a wave of sound from the west and Rolf spun around, throwing his field glasses up to his eyes.

The Russians were surging forward onto the pontoon bridges that were only just then being secured on the near side of the canal. Men dropped one after another to sharpshooter bullets but the tide was unstoppable. Rolf could see the rabid fierceness on their faces even from this distance as they charged around and over their fallen and falling compatriots with complete disregard for the danger. Only the fact that they were crossing the last real barrier between them and the government quarter, the heart of their hated foe, mattered at this point.

Rolf waved his arms furiously at the tank commanders. "The bridges! The bridges!" He pointed with both hands westward. "Take out the bridges!"

The nearest tank's commander's eyes grew wide. He ducked down in his hatch, shouting, and a moment later the turret spun around and fired.

There was a splash alongside the pontoons, followed by another and another as the rest of Nordland opened up, but the impacts only caused waves that bobbed the bridges unpredictably and made it impossible for the tanks to land a hit. Red soldiers poured across into the Tiergarten, staggering onto the near shore and diving for cover behind fallen trees and dead comrades, pushing out their bridgehead by sheer numbers. Even eighty-eight millimeter rounds from the guns atop the flak tower weren't enough to slow down the oozing green wave of destruction.

"No good!" Rolf waved off the gunners. There was no point wasting ammunition now. "Fall back! Fall back!"

Fournier started loping back from the far end of the line. Rolf cupped his hands around his mouth. "Fournier! Get the boys out of the building! Get them out of here!"

Fournier nodded and altered course to round the funkpanzer. It seemed an eternity for the Frenchman to get to the buildings on their left flank, and for a long moment Rolf stopped breathing when a shell landed between them and obscured Rolf's view.

But Fournier made it. It could not have been more than two or three minutes before the boys were pouring out of doors and windows and piling into the delivery trucks that had been pressed into service for them, but it took conscious effort by then for Rolf to unclench his teeth.

Once he was sure Fournier and his 'old men and boys' were safely on their way he turned to sprint for the funkpanzer, but he slipped in the muck and sprawled awkwardly on his face. This time his habitual clumsiness saved him, though, as a burst of machine-gun fire ripped through the air only inches over his head.

Fournier was not as fortunate. In his fervor to get back to the tracks he made the mistake of crossing over a rise instead of circling behind it and the Soviet bullets cut him nearly in half.

Rolf stared only for a second before scrambling up and into Eemi's track. He slammed the hatch closed and fell into one of the seats, not really registering as Eemi threw the track into reverse and spun around to follow the rest of Nordland's survivors back to the Chancellery.

IX

A RDELL STORMED back to Müller's office and consoled himself by skimming through the Gestapo chief's dossiers and pulling out anything that looked incriminating, compromising, or just plain interesting, and shoving them into a valise.

There was a clatter behind him and he turned to see one of Müller's adjutants stagger into the room.

"You're drunk!" Ardell observed.

"And you're detective material!" the other man countered, and guffawed.

Ardell scowled. Obviously, the comment had only been out of surprise. "I only said that because you know how Müller is about that kind of thing!"

The adjutant blew a raspberry but still plucked at his tunic as if he were trying to make himself presentable. "Whatever." He sat heavily in Müller's chair and propped his feet on the desk. He squinted at Ardell. "What in the hell are you doing? Working?"

Ardell eased the file drawer shut for safety's sake. "Just collating some files."

The adjutant shook his head. "Forget that, friend... better things to do..."

Ardell looked askance at the adjutant, fully playing the part of a dedicated Party member, and put a hint of disdain in his voice. "Oh?"

The other man nodded and belched. "You should head down to the dining hall. Big party going on there!"

Ardell was confused. There had been a lot of powerful emotions apparent among the Chancellery's denizens since he had arrived, but joviality had certainly not been one of them. "Party? Why is there a party? And if there's a party, what are *you* doing up *here*?"

The adjutant produced a wine bottle from his trouser pocket, uncorked it, and smirked. "Meeting someone!" He held out his hands in front of him as if he were holding a girl's hips and moved them in a bouncing motion over his lap. "And why is there a party? Don't you know?"

"Know what?" The air began to feel heavy in the room.

"Because it's our last chance! The Reds have crossed the Landwehr!" The adjutant laughed, too loudly, and took a long drink.

Crossed the canal? That meant only the length of the Tiergarten stood between Stalin's troops and the Government district. The final clock was truly ticking. "What about the defenders?" He thought about Rolf and the empty barracks. "How bad is it?"

"Well...." The adjutant belched again, more loudly, and took another drink. "Frau Goebbels just came up from the bunker howling about the end of the world, if that tells you anything."

"The bunker...." The walls shuddered from a heavy salvo striking near the Reichtag. Ardell closed up his valise. "I've got to get down there."

"That smelly wet hole? What the hell for?"

Ardell lifted the valise to eye level. "I have more files to collect."

"Brother, forget the files!" The adjutant waved a dismissive hand. "In a few hours it isn't going to matter anyway. You should get yourself to the dining room instead." He cupped his hands under his chest and leered at Ardell. "Lots of women down there! And not enough dresses, if you know what I mean!" He leaned back and laughed hard at his own joke, then took another drink and sat back, suddenly morose.

Ardell slipped past him, snatching his overcoat on the way out.

"They won't let you in—" were the last words he heard from the adjutant as he ran into the hall.

Ardell spun down the stairwell to the RSD office.

The door was ajar, that half-openness that spoke volumes of panicked disregard. It did nothing for Ardell's confidence.

In the office the waiting area was empty except for two chairs, one of which was turned over. The space behind the counter was just as devoid of life. Only the scattered papers littering the floor indicated anyone had been there recently.

Ardell scowled and dodged around the counter. Sounds of shuffling and muttered curses emanated from the left hand office, so he turned his attention there.

Poking his head in the door he found Meyer pushing a small painting into a satchel. An array of small but obviously valuable trinkets littered his desk. The man stopped and looked up at the sound of Ardell's entry, and the look on his face was, if anything, extremely annoyed.

Ardell locked eyes and made a point of not looking at the loot on Meyer's desk. "Trudy!" he said breathlessly. "Have you seen Miss Heffenbach?"

Meyer rolled his eyes. Ardell wondered if it was irritation at the level of emergency for which he was being disturbed, or the likely debauchery he was sure on which Ardell was intent.

"No. Have you tried the dining hall?"

Debauchery, then. "No, I haven't. So she isn't here?"

Meyer coolly folded a light civilian suit jacket into a small bundle and placed it carefully atop the satchel's contents. "I thought I made that clear?"

"Right, you did. Excuse me." Ardell backed out of the office and headed back into the hallway.

He took a moment to collect his thoughts. Surely Galya knew the tactical situation. There was every reason to believe she was already off to the bunker, and the fact that she hadn't sent for him annoyed him to no end. His best bet was to get there himself as fast as he could before things started happening without him.

He went back up the stairwell to the second floor. Staying on this level and taking the Marble Hall to the far end of the complex, with its expansive windows open to soviet snipers a bare few blocks away, would be suicide.

Running the length of the second-floor hall seemed to take forever, and he was fairly out of breath when he got to the stairwell on the eastern end. Back on the ground floor he dashed past the dining hall and stopped long enough to see that, yes, the adjutant had been right about the party, the women, and the dress count.

Beyond the dining hall the corridor turned left. He passed offices of the east wing, then a cut-through of the Old

Chancellery building, and finally reached the stairwell into the *Vorbunker*.

At the bottom of the stairs, he pulled up short. Galya was not there. This didn't surprise him but did little for his adrenaline level.

But Fengeler *was* there, sternly giving orders to the two guards who clearly were wishing they were somewhere else.

"No one is allowed in. *No one.* Unless they have express orders from Herr Goebbels, or myself. Understood?"

"Understood, Herr Colonel," they answered together.

Fengeler turned and nearly ran into Ardell. "You?" His voice was heavy with disdain. "What do you want?"

Ardell thought fast. "Colonel Fengeler. I thought I would find you here. I would like to offer you my apologies." He put out his hand, but Fengeler ignored it.

"Apologies? For what?"

"For the inquiry with Herr Müller," Ardell offered affably. "I was just doing what I felt was my duty." He dropped his hand. "You understand, I hope?"

Fengeler adjusted his cuffs and folded his arms. "Do you even know the meaning of the word 'duty', Herr Klugmann?"

"I'd like to think so. But you should know, there's a mob up in the dining hall that I fear do not."

"What do you mean, a mob?"

"Soldiers, Herr Colonel. Our soldiers!" He allowed a little righteous outrage to slip into his voice and shook his head in mock dismay. "Carrying on most disgracefully with the flower of Berlin's youth while the Reds advance! And *drunk!*"

Fengeler narrowed his eyes but did not move.

"If you listen closely," Ardell added, "you can hear the music, the laughing…"

Ardell cocked his ear and was rewarded by the two guards doing so as well. Fengeler's gaze drifted toward the stairs behind Ardell.

Suddenly he turned to one of the guards. "Go see what's happening up there."

Ardell cleared his throat suggestively as the soldier shouldered his weapon and edged past him.

Fengeler's irritation was evident. "Do you have something to add?"

"Well, sir, I would only suggest, after what we discussed upstairs, that you see for yourself."

"I do not have the time."

"With all due respect, sir, I fear the time will have to be made. I feel the influence of rank will be required."

Fengeler studied Ardell and finally shrugged in resignation. "You may be right. You should come with me. After all, I am SS and you are Gestapo. It may take us both, no?"

He waved the guard back to his place and started up the stairs, pausing only long enough to make sure Ardell was firmly in tow.

In the dining hall Fengeler waded into the festivities like an outraged father. He stormed through the crowd, overturning gramophones and bellowing curses and orders at the top of his lungs. His face was purple and at times his voice cracked with the emotion he was clearly feeling and, apparently, had little experience in managing. Ardell strolled casually in his wake, looking with bemusement at the sudden chagrin on the faces of the men and shame on those of the girls. The latter hurriedly stooped to gather what clothes they could as Fengeler herded them all into lines, men on one side and women on the other.

"Herr Klugmann!" Ardell realized Fengeler had been calling his name several times.

"Yes, Herr Colonel?"

"Take charge of the women!"

"At once, Herr Colonel." Ardell spread his hands as if he were herding sheep and ushered the ladies toward the Mosaic Hall.

They spilled into the once-impressive, red-marbled room, stepping over debris with shoes and skirts in hand, trying to keep their balance while they slung brassiere straps over their shoulders.

Ardell pushed through the gaggle to the front, turned around and scanned the line. *This must be what it's like to be a Broadway producer,* he thought. His eyes came to rest on a proud-looking middle-aged matron with a Nazi party pin dangling from the lapel of her unbuttoned jacket.

"Frau Lily?" he said with some incredulity.

Lily sniffed indignantly and swayed slightly on her feet. "Do not presume to judge me, Herr Klugmann."

"I wouldn't dare!" He stepped close. "Have you seen Trudy? Is she here?"

Lily cocked an eyebrow and shook her head. "No, *sir.*" There was a knowing tone in the way she said 'sir'. "She said something about being called to the bunker."

Ardell scowled. "That figures." He fumed for a moment, then squared his shoulders and addressed Lily loudly. "Frau Lily! How could you have allowed these young ladies to behave in such a fashion? You should be ashamed of yourself!"

Lily was suddenly sober. "But Herr Klugmann! You must be joking! The Reds—they're nearly here! The girls are terrified!"

"Nevertheless, I am holding you responsible for what happens to them!" Then Ardell frowned sympathetically and leaned in close again, dropping his voice. "Just get them dressed and get them out of here. I have bigger things to see to."

Ardell was not surprised at all when he got back to the bottom of the stairs into the bunker and found Galya there. She was defiantly glaring at the guards, who were shaking their heads at her with aplomb.

Ardell trotted up behind Galya and draped his arm over her shoulders. "Trudy! There you are, darling! I've been looking all over for you! Are you ready to meet him?"

Galya wisely assumed a hurt expression. "I was all set to go in, but they say I can't." She inclined her chin at the guards, who now seemed more apologetic with Ardell's arrival.

Ardell took the opportunity to flash his Gestapo fob at them. "You might be better off at the party, soldier."

The apparently-less-intelligent one cleared his throat nervously. "With all due respect, sir... Colonel Fengeler is up there."

"And I am down here," he answered coldly, then assumed a more congenial tone. "And the young lady... well, she has looked forward to this for days, haven't you, my dear?"

Galya turned doe eyes on the guards and nodded.

The two guards regarded the fob, then each other. Shell fire rumbled somewhere overhead and dust drifted down.

Finally, the smarter one slung his rifle on his shoulder and settled his helmet more comfortably on his head. "That's it, Hermann, I'm done," he said to his counterpart. "See you tomorrow when the war's over." He pushed past Ardell and trudged up the stairs.

Hermann watched him go, looked at Ardell and Galya, shrugged and followed.

Ardell and Galya moved swiftly through the Vorbunker. It wasn't really like he had visualized, all grim-looking concrete walls dripping with moisture and covered with Nazi regalia. The regalia was there, to be sure, but so were a number of bright paintings that Ardell was sure had probably come from the Louvre and had obviously been placed with an eye toward cheering the place up. The walls were even painted a restful pale green, and there was no dampness anywhere.

Neither were there any people. This seemed odd, given this was literally the beating heart of the Reich, but only served to indicate the immediacy of what was happening in the lower bunker. It also served their purpose as they weren't required to explain their presence to anyone.

It only took a few moments to reach the stairwell to the lower bunker. As they reached the bottom and exited into the main hallway, they encountered their first sign of life: the bald head of Heinz Linge, Hitler's personal valet. He was just stepping out of Der Führer's office and, before he could look

142

up with his deep-set eyes, Ardell and Galya dodged to the left into the main bathroom.

They slipped into separate stalls as the sound of Linge's shuffling footsteps approached and stopped. There was a sound of a metal door being swung, then a slam and a heavy click as the latch was thrown.

The agents climbed up onto their respective commodes as the footsteps entered the lavatory and passed down the row of stalls and back again. The treads paused again by the door, then the lights went out, followed by a lighter slam as the bathroom door was closed.

After a moment Ardell crept noiselessly out of his stall to find Galya already by the sinks, examining a small map by flashlight. He looked over her shoulder and she pointed to a spot on the paper, then to a dark corner beyond the stalls.

"There's a door to Hitler's sitting room there," she whispered. "That's our in." She drew her pistol, doused the light, and they felt along the wall toward the corner.

With the sealing of the stairwell door Linge finished his rounds and returned to Hitler's office.

Joseph Goebbels was there, sitting nonchalantly on the desk. He was acting as if he hadn't a care in the world, but Linge knew it was, as it had ever been, an act. Martin

Bormann was there as well, pug-faced and anxious, pacing, while sitting hunched over in a chair the cadaverous Doctor Stumpfegger , Hitler's personal physician, watched the other two with clinical disinterest.

It was this latter figure Linge sidled up to. The doctor looked up and cocked an eyebrow.

"The bunker is clear, Herr Doctor."

Stumpfegger's brow did not relent. "Did you check the ventilation room? The electrical room? What of the bathrooms?"

"I checked everywhere," Linge grumbled. "No one is here. They're all upstairs plotting their escape."

It was almost a scene from a Stooges short—the bathroom door slinking open, Ardell peeking within cautiously, Galya appearing above him—except there was no audience chuckling in the background.

The scene in Hitler's sitting room was no less creepy: thick carpets had been laid at one point to give a homey atmosphere, so much as could be accomplished. Now they served mostly to muffle sound and deaden the already heavy air. There was a couch, not a classy, elegant piece or even a gaudy flamboyant fixture, but rather a tawdry print-pattern that Ardell would have expected to see in his grandmother's parlor, a pair of matching chairs, and a desk. Somewhere off to his right a clock ticked.

On the couch a young blond reclined as if sleeping. Ardell identified her from his briefing photos as Eva, Hitler's mistress, but her identity would have been clear regardless; leaning over her was the one man who had been responsible for so much death and misery—Hitler himself. There was the trademark toothbrush mustache, the side-parted hair, the simple gray tunic and boots.

But the man!

His eyes were sunken, bloodshot, and vacant. His posture was stooped, even allowing for the fact he was leaning over the girl. When he straightened Ardell could see his tunic was stained and be-crumbed, and his left hand shook with a coarse tremor. This was what was left of the charisma-drenched dynamo of recrimination and vengeance that had launched a war. Now he was just a shell.

Hitler reached out and softly stroked Eva's hair but she did not stir. Ardell knew she wouldn't—he could smell the telltale burnt scent of cyanide in the air.

Hitler turned toward a side table where a silver tray bore a pistol and a small white capsule.

This is it, Ardell thought. He drew his own pistol and started to raise it.

Suddenly Galya snatched him back and eased the door shut in one swift motion. "No!" she hissed. "This is perfect! He needs to do it himself!"

"What are you saying?" Ardell breathed back. "Better for the Germans if we do it and they know it!"

"You don't know what you're saying! If he does it—"

"He goes down a martyr!"

"But if word gets out the OSS did it there will be civil war between the Nazi holdouts and Allied sympathizers!"

"And that would just be too much for Uncle Joe to handle, would it?"

"Is that all you can think about? Politics? What about the lives of innocent civilians?"

"You mean the innocent civilians that voted this guy into office?"

"They didn't know what they were getting themselves into!"

"Now you sound like my father! They didn't read his book!"

"Whoever bothers to read a book!" Galya clenched her fists. "You're so damned obstinate! Always having to be in control!"

"Me in control? You've been calling the shots since I found you. You wouldn't even be in here if it weren't for me! If I hadn't come along when I did—"

"Fine!" Galya growled through clenched teeth. "Let's just give him a minute. If he doesn't take the pill—"

The door yanked open, and Hitler was there, rheumy eyes wide with shock.

They stared at each other for a heartbeat, then Hitler's eyes filled with rage and he opened his mouth to shout. Like a predatory cat Galya reacted, slapping him across the face with her left hand and bringing up her pistol with her right.

She fired one round, and Hitler was dead.

In the office the gunshot reverberated like a thunderclap. Even Goebbels seemed caught by surprise that it had actually happened.

Linge watched the propaganda minister the most intently so as to etch this moment into his mind. Goebbels' vulture-like upper lip hardly twitched once the initial jolt abated. There was no following tremble of emotion, no jaw-clenching of grim determination, no squaring of the shoulders in resolution, only a calculating glance around the room as if to be sure it was finally time for whatever he was planning next.

Linge took a step toward the sitting room door but Stumpfegger reached up and laid a hand on his chest to stop him. "Wait. Give it a minute or two."

Linge looked down at him, confused.

"In case," Stumpfegger went on, "it was a poor shot."

Hitler lay on the threshold of the bathroom door, only a faint trickle of blood oozing from the bullet hole in his temple.

Ardell blew out a breath and looked at Galya with irritation. "I was going to do that."

Galya likewise exhaled sharply and shook her head as if she was waking from a dream. "That was too quick."

If Ardell hadn't known her as well as he had he would have probably misunderstood her remark, but he only frowned even deeper. "You're not right, you know."

She flashed him a look. "Help me get him up on the couch."

"Why?"

"Make it look like a suicide, of course!"

"Are you still on about that?"

"Just do it, will you? They'll be in here any second!"

"Are we going to have this argument again? The last time we did a man died!"

"Since when were you a comedian? If they don't think it's a suicide, they'll come looking for us!"

Unfortunately, he couldn't argue with her logic. He grunted to himself, holstered his pistol and dragged Hitler up onto the couch opposite Eva.

"Stop muttering, Delly, they'll hear you!" She fussed over his placement for a moment and then nodded to herself. "Good enough. Let's go!" She tiptoed to the door.

He gave her a look at least as aggravated as the one she had given him, snatched the pistol off the tray, dropped the clip and pocketed a round.

Galya turned when she realized Ardell was not behind her. "What are you doing now?"

"You want it to look like a suicide, don't you?"

The door handle started turning.

"Come on, Delly!"

Ardell replaced the clip, dropped the pistol on the couch, and darted through the bathroom door, pausing only long enough to fling Galya's bullet casing toward the bodies.

Once back inside the bathroom they reclaimed their places atop the commodes as they waited for the voices beyond the door to subside.

Oddly enough not all the voices seemed upset.

X

TWILIGHT FILTERED through dust-choked air into Fengeler's office through a single north-facing window. The shelling was constant now, rattling doors and knocking plaster from the ceilings. Despite this Fengeler stood calmly in his shirtsleeves, sorting papers from his satchel into several stacks on his desk.

Galya stepped quickly in, breathless from the climb up the stairs. "You sent for me, Herr Colonel?"

Fengeler hardly glanced up. "Where have you been?"

Galya assumed a demur air. "My apologies, Herr Colonel. My services have been... much in demand."

Fengeler looked over her atypically rumpled clothing and mussed hair and snorted. "Doubtless. Did you come from the music hall?"

"No, sir. I was in the Vorbunker."

If he disbelieved her, he was good enough at hiding it. "Here." He lifted a stack of papers and held them out to her. "These need catalogued."

She took them without a word, found herself a seat at a small worktable, and started making a list of the documents. A nearby blast rattled the window but Fengeler only pulled another pile of papers and continued sorting, unperturbed.

Galya looked up from her work. "You seem very relaxed, Herr Colonel."

"Does that surprise you?"

"Everyone else is afraid."

"Do you think I should be?"

Galya paused, careful about the impression she was giving Fengeler. "I'm sorry, sir. That's not what I meant to say." She put her face back into her list and allowed Fengeler to occupy himself unmolested.

After several minutes, though, he broke the silence. "I had a sister once. She joined the Communists in 1932, took up living in Zavod."

Galya continued working but cocked an ear carefully.

"Herr Ribbentrop had just signed the pact with the Soviets." His voice held an audible sneer at the last word. "We were just finishing in Tibet and were heading back home. It should have been a safe enough journey... I asked permission to make a slight detour to collect her, to bring her home."

He paused while he examined another paper closely, grabbed a pen and made a correction, then put it in its pile.

"But when I arrived their Mongol KGB chief couldn't seem to grasp what I needed to do. He didn't *agree* that it was necessary for me to take her back home, to get her out of that warren, and his feral suspicion of me led us to a confrontation that left my sister dead."

Somewhere a few blocks away there was small arms fire and shouting.

"It was then that I saw that the *Rus,* once a great race of Vikings, had lost their former proud bearing and in fact any capability of rational thought." He straightened in his chair and handed another sheaf to Galya. "They had been defiled by decadent cultures and degenerate blood. Their humanity had bred out. You can tell," he nodded out the window to where the cries were raising in intensity, "by the way they throw themselves at us with no regard for the lives of their fellows, or anything but the most simplistic tactics."

He caught Galya's eye, but the glance he gave her was cold and flat. "Therefore, what is there to fear?"

He stood, donned his tunic and collected his cap. "Get those to Sergeant Hechner in the motor pool. He has a plane on the Tiergarten." He glanced out the window where smoke shrouded the Reichtag. Over his shoulder Galya thought she caught a glimpse of red fluttering from the top of the building.

Apparently Fengeler saw it as well, for he took a sharp breath. "But I would suggest you hurry," he said as he left.

Galya watched him go. She placed the papers in an envelope, sealed it, and dropped it into a dustbin before walking out the other way.

By nightfall the outer offices of the Chancellery were untenable. Not only were all the windows shattered, allowing the cold dampness in unabated, but any movement was almost guaranteed to catch the eye of Russian snipers that had caused such devastation in Stalingrad and were now making their way into the upper floors of the surrounding apartment blocks.

Thus it was that General Wilhelm Mohnke, the young, pinched-faced Battle Commander of the government district, was holding his last conference in the relative, if only temporary, safety of the basement.

He waited impatiently, seated on a table, while most of the high ranking officers and their functionaries filed in from the upper floors. Behind him a large map of the city center had been tacked up on the concrete wall and furiously marked with red lines and arrows showing the ever-shrinking boundaries of the Reich.

Rolf filed in behind a wide-eyed Luftwaffe general and took a seat towards the back. His eyes were sunken and his face was drawn, and the rumpled state of his uniform let everyone know without having to be told just how bad things were 'out there'.

Next came a smattering of staff officers, most of whom twittered amongst themselves like schoolgirls at their first dance, though with an even more desperate edge as they checked the map and realized just how close the war had finally come.

Meyer appeared in the doorway with Lily and Galya and edged past the staff flunkies. He seated the women at the front to take notes and settled himself in at the left edge of the map.

Müller arrived then with Ardell in tow. Though the Gestapo chief found himself a seat in the front row, Ardell excused himself when he spotted Rolf, and circled around the entire group to stand against the wall just behind his father. Rolf watched him but said nothing, and Ardell obligingly returned the favor.

Mohnke paced faster as the last few attendees trickled in. From where he was standing Ardell caught snatches of conversations—what had been heard (or, in fact, hadn't been heard) from the Reichtag, whether or not Wenck had actually succeeded in breaking through from the west or had simply given up and gone over to the Americans, and—the hottest topic of all—what was the significance of high-ranking staff saluting a gasoline fire that had been set in the Chancellery garden late that afternoon.

Finally, Mohnke picked up a gavel and rapped on the table. "*Achtung!*"

Everyone got to their feet and saluted, but the 'Heil Hitlers' seemed less pervasive.

If Mohnke noticed, he let it go. "Please be seated." Once the room had resettled, he took a deep breath and plunged right into it.

"You men represent the best of the leadership of the Reich. I am going to ask you to exercise that leadership one last time. We have two hundred and fifty men, officers and civilians remaining in the Chancellery, and the time has come—" He swallowed hard before finishing, "to abandon the city."

An excited buzz began amongst the audience but Mohnke barreled on before it could gain any real momentum. He picked up a sheaf of papers from the table. "We will be splitting up into ten groups. I will take charge of the first group, General Rattenhuber the second, Herr Naumann the third, and the rest of you I have assigned here." He glared around the room to quiet the murmurs and continued. "We will make for the U-bahn to pass under the Soviet lines." He turned to the map and indicated a spot to the east of the Chancellery. "Our first checkpoint will be the entrance at Kaiserhof, here."

One senior officer raised his hand. "Excuse me, General? Won't the Reds be watching the tunnels? It's an obvious escape route."

Mohnke shook his head. "The Soviets have been avoiding them out of fear they've been mined. It's the safest route we have."

"But Kaiserhof is a hundred meters away... towards the Reds! The snipers—"

"We will, of course, have to do this under cover of darkness. Tonight. And we will have to maintain separation so as not to attract attention. We will set out at midnight and groups will depart at ten-minute intervals thereafter."

An older staff officer stood. "And what about after? Once we reach the tunnels? Where do we go?"

Mohnke's shoulders seemed to sag. "Once we are clear of the city we are to head for the Elbe."

This time the agitation could not be quelled. "We will surrender to the Americans?" the first officer sputtered. "We will not regroup? We have to regroup—"

Whatever other exhortations he was trying to utter were drowned out as more men stood and started arguing, protesting, or agreeing. Finally Meyer climbed up on the table and started waving his hands angrily. "Silence! Silence! *Let the general speak!*"

The contention gradually subsided, helped along by the rumbling of Russian shells filtering through from above.

Mohnke looked over the room with cold eyes. "Perhaps it would be best," he grated, "if I shared with you General Weidling's brief." He pulled a page from his sheaf, cleared his throat, and once he was sure he had everyone's undivided attention, began reading.

"By order of General Helmuth Weidling, Commander, Berlin Defense Area.

"Active position fighting shall cease at twenty-three hundred hours tonight, whereupon all troops must be prepared to break through the Red Army's ring now closing around Berlin."

Ardell thought it ironic that Weidling wrote as if the Russians were only just then making their way into the city, and were not actually closing their fingers around Berlin's very throat.

Mohnke continued. "We must attempt this in small battle groups, probing for weak areas wherever we can find them. Our general compass direction will be northwest toward Neuruppin. If you get that far..."

Mohnke looked around. All eyes were on him and it seemed as though the very room was holding its breath.

"If you get that far, keep moving.

"This is a general order. There are no more specific details. No provision can be made for any rear guard."

Mohnke set the paper on the table.

"We *are* the rear guard."

Over the next few hours people started gathering in the sparsely-lit garage under the east end of the Chancellery complex. First the civilians arrived, standing about awkwardly in hastily-donned military tunics and boots, frankly terrified at the thought of being pulled into what they expected was a front-line military operation. Then the staffers collected, who at least had had some level of military training and so felt some confidence they would know how to handle themselves, though they, too, were apprehensive about the prospect of actually seeing the enemy face-to-face. Then the hardened veterans trickled in as they were able to disengage from their defensive positions in the upper floors or surrounding structures. They were nervous as well, but for entirely different reasons—they knew this was anything but a proper mission. There was no real command chain, no discussion of ammunition or fuel supplies, no tactical objectives or coordination with other units; only the daunting task of shepherding panicky non-combatants in small ineffective bands through what they knew for a fact was the most demanding combat environment they had ever faced.

Mohnke and several of his aides arrived and started filtering through the milling crowd, whispering encouragement and separating them into small groups. Rolf stood separate from the others and smoked his next-to-last Juno. Just a little to his right a large shell hole in the wall beckoned all comers into a night marked with smoky fires and flashing barrages. The sound of fighting was very close now.

Soon individual faces started appearing out of the crowd to join him. Eemi was the first, followed by a clutch of Nordland Pioneers and a few men Rolf recognized from their recon company.

"Evening, sir," Eemi offered. He folded his arms across his chest and shivered. "Got chilly since sunset."

Rolf watched the crowd carefully. He was more than a little worried that he hadn't seen any of his tank crews. Eemi watched him, looking for a response, and when he got none eased the roster out of Rolf's hand. He looked it over and scoffed.

"Group Ten! Figures! Last ones out. The snipers will know for certain something's up by the time we get going."

Rolf still said nothing, but this time it was because he had spotted Ardell weaving his way toward him. His son stopped an arm's length away and Rolf put out his cigarette.

"I don't recall seeing your name in my group," he said, probably more flippantly than he intended, but it was hard to keep the hurt out of his voice. "Are you here to make sure I keep my end of the bargain?"

"I'm happy to see you as well, Captain," Ardell snapped. "And for the record, I kept *my* end."

Rolf immediately regretted his accusatory tone. There was every possibility these would be the last words he would ever say to this man, his son, whom he hadn't seen for ten years and had missed every single day, and it wasn't right that he should allow the bitterness of their parting, and the difficulty of their few encounters over these last days, spoil what time they had left.

He took a deep breath and worked hard to keep his tone even and, he sincerely hoped, genuine. The trouble is he never really had known what constituted a 'genuine' tone, so he opted for softness, which was easier to achieve. "That's all right... you're welcome to join us."

This didn't get much of a response from Ardell, who only continued to look past Rolf to the shell hole, but at least he nodded an acknowledgment of the invitation.

Rolf turned away and Ardell decided this would be a good time to take stock of his other travel companions. Before he could really look them over, though, there was a slight stir at the rear of the group and the men parted to make room for Galya, who was wearing a dark military tunic over her white blouse. Ardell took a step back to get out of her way but stopped when she closed the distance to him anyway.

She spared only the barest of glances between him and Rolf but Ardell knew she had sized up their situation completely in that fraction of a second. "I honestly didn't expect to find your tanker here."

"Why not?"

"I thought he was all about *Ein Volk, Ein Reich, Ein Führer?*"

"He's always been more like a *Deutchland Uber Alles* kind of guy." He stared at Rolf's back for a long moment, then turned back to Galya. "Hey... didn't I see your name on Meyer's list?"

She cocked her head at him. "You know, you're a real jerk when you're fighting with your dad."

Ardell exhaled and looked away. *I don't have time for this,* he thought. *Or the energy.*

But Galya was still speaking. "But yes, you did, and I admire your skills of observation. But I'd be safer with the Reds than with him." She made a groping motion with her hands.

Ardell furrowed his brow. "You talk as if you're not a Russian yourself."

Galya looked, Ardell was surprised to see, genuinely offended. "I'm *not* Russian, Delly. I'm Ukraine. I thought you knew that."

"There's a difference?"

"Oh, I'm sorry!" she said in a mocking tone. "I thought you were Canadian?" She leaned back on one hip and crossed her arms. "Don't ever call me Russian again."

"Sorry. What's the beef, though? Did they do something to you?"

"To the Ukraine. We call it the Holodomor."

Somewhere in Ardell's memory a tinkling bell rang. "Wait a minute... I remember my mom talking about that. It was actually a part of the fight that caused..." he glanced over at Rolf, who was talking to a younger man about making sure they kept a good interval after Group Nine so the snipers' guard would slip. "Wasn't it a famine or something?"

"Not hardly. Just a despot wanting to prove a point." Galya sat heavily on a folding chair and looked around at all the Nazi uniforms surrounding them. "It's funny, in a tragic way. We thought the Germans would liberate us from the Russians."

"But they turned out to be worse?"

"No. Only different."

"So if you hate Stalin so much, why do you work for him?"

"It put me in the front lines. Gave me a chance to make contacts, find opportunities. I knew eventually I would be able to slip away."

"You became an agent just to escape?" Ardell found this hard to believe. *Talk about taking the hard road...* "Your childhood must have been more messed up than I realized."

Galya nodded more to herself, and when she spoke her voice was distant. "Growing up was... painful. My father had a hard time adjusting to life after the Revolution. It was easier to drink and blame others. But the only other people around were my mother, and me."

"And your mother didn't do anything about it?" He had an image in his mind of what her mother must have been like to create someone as hard-edged as Galya, and couldn't reconcile that with someone meekly submissive to an abusive drunkard.

"My mother was strict, and judgmental. But she was weak when push... when push..." She looked at Ardell expectantly.

"Push came to shove."

"Yes, that." She took a deep breath. "And there was too much pushing and shoving."

Ardell reached out and squeezed her shoulder. "Sounds like you had more than one reason to leave... I'm sorry."

"Don't pity me, Delly. It is what it is."

"But look at what it's going to be! When you get back to the States and word gets around that you killed—"

"No!" She cried, loud enough to draw a few glances from those nearby. She stepped in close and dropped her voice to a whisper. "No one must ever know what happened down there. *No one!*"

"Why?" Now Ardell was truly mystified. "You'd be famous. You'd be set for life!"

"And the Secret Police would know I ran and my parents would suffer."

"Suffer? But I thought... your parents..."

"What? That I hated them? I did, Delly, for a long, long time. But then I got out here," she waved a hand around, "and I began to realize what it meant to be a person, just a simple human being, in impossible circumstances. Would I have done any better, in their place? I don't know." She noticed the confused look on Ardell's face and laid a hand on his cheek. "I did hate them. I don't now. No, I don't agree with how they handled things, and I don't want to go back to them, but they're still my parents. They still deserve that respect."

It took Ardell a long moment to even begin to process what seemed to be her frankly contradictory attitudes. Finally, he decided to put it on the back burner for the moment. "So what are you going to do? Not going home, not going to the States...?"

"I'm going to go to Switzerland. Going to fade into the scenery."

"Won't the Secret Police come looking for you anyway?"

She reached up again, but this time patted him on the cheek like a small child. "Delly, Delly, there are millions missing in action on the Eastern Front. *Millions.* Just missing, with no trace of their existence but a name on a list. What's one more?"

Ardell shook his head, still trying to make sense of it, and noticed a very young lad of no more than fifteen or sixteen talking intently to Rolf. The boy was clearly not a civilian in a borrowed uniform; his attire was more deliberately fitted, and proudly displayed an Iron Cross on the breast.

Ardell edged closer to listen in. The boy was speaking, nervously but firmly, with his chin held high, though Ardell could see it trembling.

"—the word from your tank commanders, sir, is that, with all due respect, they won't be coming."

"They won't—" The shock in Rolf's voice was evident despite the fact he had his back to Ardell. "Did they say why, Private Schenk?"

"They said they would rather fight their way out with their tanks than scrabble in the tunnels like rats." The boy swallowed hard. "Sir."

Rolf stared intently at the boy until he shuffled from one foot to the other. "That figures," he breathed finally. "Stubborn and proud to the last."

"It will be their last." It was nearly a whole second before Ardell realized he had said that out loud.

Rolf turned and looked Ardell up and down. "Perhaps. Perhaps not. A Tiger's a formidable weapon."

Ardell's lip curled up on one side. "Have you seen the columns moving in?"

Rolf's expression darkened. "Only from one end." He turned back to the young private. "Wolfgang. You should come with us."

"Begging your pardon, sir, but my place is here. Defending the city."

"Defending the—" Once again Rolf was dumbstruck. "But there's nothing left to defend!"

"I still want to fight, sir! I still want to do my part!"

"Your part is to rebuild after!"

"But if they destroy us, what will be the use of rebuilding?"

Rolf had nothing to say to this, and after an awkward moment the young private adjusted the set of his rifle on his shoulder, took a step back, came to attention and saluted. "I must be going now, sir. Excuse me." He turned and disappeared into the crowd.

At last midnight rolled around. The sound of gunfire had fallen away an hour before, right on schedule, as the Nazi war machine had begun to face reality.

Somewhere in the garage a whistle blew and General Mohnke led his group to the shell hole in the wall. With barely a word between them, they climbed up and out, a few at a time.

Ardell watched them go, and wondered how many of their bodies he would find when it was his turn to follow them into the darkness.

XI

ROLF WATCHED the last of Group Nine set out and checked his watch. He carefully counted out ten minutes, let out a breath and looked up. "Alright, then. Our turn." He pushed off from where he had been leaning against the wall and moved to the head of his group as they gathered themselves, mentally and physically, for the journey ahead.

He assumed an easy stance and looked everyone in the eyes. *This was so much easier, when there was a clear task to handle.* "Now listen up! We move out in twos and threes. I will let you each know when it's time to go. Stay in the shadows! This is extremely important!" He looked pointedly at the civilians. "If you get the attention of the snipers you'll be the death of those behind you." He motioned Eemi to step to the front. The younger man was clearly apprehensive, but the look in his eyes underneath it all said he was ready, really ready, for it all to be over.

At least, that's what Rolf hoped he saw.

"Eemi," Rolf took another deep breath and blew it out. "Take us out."

Eemi looked to his left and right at a pair of Pioneers he had befriended over the last days and clapped them on their shoulders. They nodded to each other, stepped up to the shell hole as one, and vanished over the edge.

Over the next several minutes Rolf waved more people out, forcing himself to wait for the second hand on his watch to complete three full revolutions between each team. Some went out eagerly, some needed coaxing, but at least all of them managed to get clear of the immediate area. At least there were no sounds of bullets striking or wounded screaming.

Finally only Rolf, Galya and Ardell remained. Rolf looked around at the empty garage, marveling at the damage the building had sustained and thinking about the looks on the faces of those he had sent out just now. *We hadn't foreseen this,* he lamented to himself, *back in Thirty-Three. Everyone had been so full of hope... things had been so bad, they could only get better. And for a time, they did.*

He wondered if Margaret had been right, about the natural traits of absolute rulers. She had worried the Soviets were a type and the Nazis would follow suit, but he was sure they wouldn't, they were a different breed, weren't they? But then he had seen how the determination to make something of Germany once again led to the horrible things he had witnessed at Leningrad, and Oranienbaum, and the Courland Pocket. He had tried to excuse those things in his mind as the random unapproved acts of soldiers lacking discipline or supervision, but when he finally arrived in Berlin and saw what the leaders themselves were doing, hiding in holes and making grand speeches about 'sacrifice' and 'noble last stands' while stringing up children and old women for cowardice, he had been forced to admit the rot had reached the very core. The Weimar had been hard to live through, but at least that had been only a matter of money—not this horrifying, willful, glorified self-immolation in the name of an ideal that had grown into a beast as reactive and uncontrollable as any Frankenstein.

Grand ideas… He scanned the wreckage around them again and nervously clenched the toy soldier in his pocket.

He sighed. There was little to be done at this point but to leave it all behind. He shrugged to himself and looked over at Galya and Ardell. "Ready?"

He stopped, confused at the startled looks on their faces. He turned toward the hole in the wall—

Fengeler was there with his death squad, smirking and holding a pistol on them with casual indifference. Rolf's heart sank when he saw his young Hitlerjugend Wolfgang standing among the thugs, and bile rose in his throat.

"When I heard this rumor of a breakout," Fengeler crowed, "I could scarcely believe my ears!" He took a step into the garage, his boys obediently staying a bare pace behind. "I recovered my men from where they had been scattered by Herr Müller's whims and led them through literally battalions of swarming Russians to see for myself, convinced I had to be wrong."

He took another step and stared Ardell in the eye. "And yet, here you are."

Rolf hesitated for only a moment. The toy soldier seemed to have suddenly turned into lead in his hand, and he had finally had enough. "Step aside, Herr Colonel. The war is over. Here, at least."

Fengeler didn't take his eyes off Ardell. "What I have seen out there argues otherwise."

"General Weidling has given the order for a breakout—"

"Yes, I am aware of what that coward uttered the moment our beloved Führer took it upon himself to extinguish his flaming brand." He turned at last to Rolf, and even he was able to see the glint of madness in the other man's eyes. "Thankfully Herr Goebbels had more sense and rescinded the directive, which I am here to enforce. Take them."

There was little point in resisting. Fengeler had at least a dozen lackeys and, for all their youth, they had enough sense to keep some of their number back out of reach to cover the prisoners with their machine pistols while the bigger ones wrestled them down and bound them. Nor had running been an option; the garage was wide open for dozens of yards in all directions and though it was littered with debris, none of it was really big enough to provide cover enough to escape.

Ardell and Galya were secured to rebars projecting from the fractured concrete walls, but Fengeler held up his boys as they took Rolf. He cast about the wreckage for a moment, and his eyes brightened when he laid them on the folding chair Galya had been occupying only minutes before. "Here!" He caught the chair with his foot and slid it towards the tanker. "Put the Captain here. Handcuff his wrists to the legs... here, above the spindle, so he can't slip off."

Once they were finished Fengeler reached a hand out to one scowling youth. "Grenade?"

The boy reached into a satchel and withdrew a small egg-shaped object and placed it in Fengeler's hand. The colonel tossed it idly in the air as he stepped up to stand in front of Rolf.

"Herr Captain. Do you know what this is?"

Rolf, of course, recognized the device as not being one of the Wermacht's ubiquitous potato mashers. But he saw no reason to play along with Fengeler's games, and he really had finally had enough.

"Captain? I said—"

"It's a Soviet F-1 grenade!"

"Yes. Yes, it is!" He held it up and turned it in his hand, examining the workmanship with disdain. "Based rather poorly on the French design, if I am not mistaken. The workmanship leaves much to be desired, to be sure, but the basic design is rather clever. See here," he pointed to the spoon-like handle secured to the tall stem on one end, "the fuse is quite different from ours. If one pulls this pin—"

Rolf heard Ardell and Galya both inhale sharply behind him.

"—the device is not armed until..." He smiled, released the handle with a twang, waited two heartbeats and tossed the grenade out the shell hole as if he were chucking bread crumbs to ducks. It exploded in the street with a ringing blast.

"Four-point-five seconds, from release of the handle to detonation. More or less," he shrugged. "It *is* Russian, after all." He reached to his trooper for another. "Here, Captain." He stooped and forced the second grenade into Rolf's right hand.

"When the Reds finally arrive and shoot you—"

He pulled the pin and stood.

"—you will drop the grenade and they will die." He pocketed the pin, smiling in smug satisfaction. "So you see, Captain, even though you refuse to carry on the fight I can still make you strike a blow for your Fatherland."

Rolf found he was breathing heavily and forced himself to calm down. He nodded to the two behind him. "What about them? Why tie them up? They're only civilians."

"Well," Fengeler glanced at Galya skeptically, but the look he gave Ardell was pure disdain. "One of them is, anyway."

"Then why not just shoot them and be done with it?"

"Hey!" Ardell spouted. "Don't be trying to do me any favors!"

Fengeler shook his head. "Oh, tsk-tsk, Herr Captain. I need them here to make sure you don't grow tired of life and set off the trap too soon." He looked up at Ardell and Galya and cocked an eyebrow. "I'm sure there's at least one of them you'd be reluctant to kill."

Seemingly satisfied that all was finally in order, Fengeler raised a finger and spun it in a circular motion as he marched away to the stairs. "Come now, my lads! Let us see who else we can inspire to resist. The barbarians are at the very gates!"

The rumble of artillery fire started picking up again, and flashes of orange light silhouetted the buildings visible across the street outside the shell hole.

"The Reds are on the move again," Ardell observed grimly. "Just the other side of the block!"

Rolf pulled uselessly at the handcuffs again. "Can one of you reach me?" he snapped. *Would have seemed the obvious move,* he grumbled. He knew he was getting agitated, but having a live grenade in one hand and bloodthirsty hordes on the other can do bad things to a person's attitude.

Galya stretched her foot out. "I'm at least a meter short." A series of blasts echoed through the garage, making them wince. Galya turned on Ardell with fire in her eyes. "They're hitting the west end of the Chancellery. Think of something!"

Ardell sighed heavily and reached his foot as well. "If you can scoot your chair to me, I can kick out the spindles and you can slip your hands off the legs."

Rolf twisted to get a look at the debris behind him, moved his feet backwards astride the chair and lifted up and back, landing heavily.

"Yeah! Just like that! Keep coming!" Rolf inched another step, and another.

The hissing scream of katyusha rockets sounded, frighteningly close this time, and a cloud of dust through the shell hole marked a wall giving way on their exit route. Rolf started and missed his footing, landing askew and falling onto his right hand. He grunted in pain and Ardell and Galya both caught their breath.

After a few ragged breaths Rolf cocked his leg sideways and pushed, leaving a bloody trail from his hand on the sharp concrete fragments littering the floor as he dragged himself closer to Ardell. "How much farther?" he panted.

"Almost there! Just a few centimeters!"

Rolf pushed harder, face screwed in pain, as machine gun fire erupted at the top of the stairs.

"There!" Ardell brought his foot down like an axe and broke the chair's legs. "That's got it!"

Rolf rolled to a sitting position, carefully took the grenade into his left hand, and stood. He limped to the shell hole and tossed the grenade out. Its detonation seemed pitiful in comparison to the near-ear-splitting blasts from the Russian field guns and mortars.

Rolf finished smashing the chair as the gunfire at the stairs drew closer.

"Draw them down here, my lads!" Fengeler's voice echoed. "We have a surprise for them!"

Rolf scrambled back to Ardell and Galya, but stopped, suddenly frozen with uncertainty. He searched their faces and looked about quickly for something sharp enough to cut rope.

"I have a knife," Galya pushed her leg out again. "In my boot. I can't reach it."

Rolf breathed a heavy sigh of relief and in a few moments had them cut loose. He glanced to the staccato flashes of light beyond the shell hole as they rubbed their wrists. "Get up! We need to go before the snipers get any more light!"

As they reached the lip of the hole Fengeler rounded the last turn of the stairwell. "Halt! *Halt, damn you!*" He fired his pistol at them, but to no avail—the three were already off into the flickering void.

The hundred meters from the shell hole eastward to the Kaiserhof U-Bahn station stretched before them. To the left loomed the battered shell of the Chancellery; to the right the few walls left of the Allgemaine Warenhandelsgesellschaft department store trembled with the echoing barrage. Piles of rubble laced with burned cars and abandoned armored vehicles complicated the route to relative safety, and Ardell was not in the least surprised to find fresh bodies among the remains of soldiers and civilians that had been trampled underfoot, tire and track for days.

They sprinted from cover to cover, doing what they could to stay out of the light of the fires that raged all around. The only saving grace from the conflagrations was the billowing smoke.

At least we have the bodies of the more careless ones to show us where the hot spots were, Ardell thought cynically.

Galya had managed to get some distance ahead of he and Rolf but was stuck behind a broken corner wall, pinned down by plinking Russian bullets from the far end of the street.

Things weren't any better for Ardell and Rolf, hunkered down behind an overturned staff car and watching Fengeler and his goons spilling out of the garage behind them. At least their pursuers were just as desperate for cover.

"Sniper ahead, and Fengeler behind," Rolf grumbled.

"You noticed."

Rolf glared at Ardell's sarcasm. "I was making sure *you* noticed. You know, sometimes it just needs to be said out loud, so we both know."

Ardell rolled his eyes at his father's literality and scrambled a short distance away to snag a rifle from a dead soldier. "I need to see where the sniper is. Without getting shot, of course." He chambered a round and put the weapon to his shoulder.

"You won't hit him from here with that!" Rolf barked.

"I don't need to hit him." Ardell snapped back. He took a deep breath and called out at the top of his lungs.

"Trudy!"

Galya remained fixed in place, focused on the street ahead.

"Trudy!" Ardell called again, with the same result.

He edged around the far end of the car, away from Rolf, cursing under his breath, and chucked a stone at Galya.

"*Galya!*"

She finally turned and Ardell gestured dramatically toward the sniper. "Throw something! Draw his fire!"

She glared back at him and spread her hands helplessly.

"Throw something! Anything! *Something* to get his attention!"

Galya scowled and untucked her blouse, slipped her brassiere out through her sleeve and tossed it out into the street.

Like Pavlov's dog the sniper took the shot. Ardell marked the gaping window frame where the muzzle had flashed, drew a bead and fired. He thought he saw a faint spark where his round struck the masonry and saw enough of a shadow ducking back under cover to be satisfied he had accomplished his goal.

"*Now! Run!*" Taking his own advice he bolted into the open, legs reaching as far and as fast as he could make them go for the subway. He overtook Galya and didn't look back to see if she or Rolf had managed to follow until he dove down the stairs to safety.

He stood in the dark, gasping for breath, and was soon joined by two other shadows gulping air just as hard.

After a few moments Ardell realized it wasn't pitch black in the station, but rather was very dimly lit by candles. The trouble was they were spread throughout a seething throng of refugees whose once-bright clothing had become dingy and shapeless after days of furtive hiding from the fighting above.

The three slid down the stairs, ears cocked for sounds of Fengeler arriving above, and pushed into the blank-faced throng. Galya led the way, with Ardell next, scanning for the exit, and Rolf brought up the rear, also looking this way and that, but for an entirely different reason.

"Eemi!" he called hoarsely, then with more conviction. "Eemi! Franz! Willi! Where are you?"

An old man looked up from a coveted seat on a bench and shook his head. "You won't find them, my boy."

Rolf continued to search the crowd. "What are you talking about?"

"I've been watching you people come through here for hours now." He shook his head and puffed on a pipe filled with something foul.

Rolf snagged Ardell's sleeve to hold him up, and he pulled Galya to a stop as well. "What of it?" Rolf asked the old man.

"The soldiers just lose their uniforms. Some get coats, hats, what-have-you, from us," he nodded at the others cowering in the dark, many of whom regarded Rolf's tunic with disdain. "Some already have them," he finished.

"Deserting?"

"Disappearing. Just... fading into the crowd."

Rolf cupped his hands to his mouth. "Lars!"

"I'm telling you, it's no use."

"You don't understand, Opa." Ardell was surprised to hear an anxious edge in Rolf's voice. "I'm responsible for them."

"Not any more you're not."

There was a loud commotion at the entry stairs as Fengeler finally made his way down the entry, shoving into the crowd like an ice-breaker.

Ardell looked around quickly. There was a car slowly coming down the tracks roughly marked with large red crosses. Shapes framed by lamplight could just be seen moving within.

Ardell impatiently took Rolf by the elbow and dragged him toward the entry step. "Give it up. It's over. For them, anyway. But we need to go!"

None of the three wanted to actually get into the hospital car, given the wails and cries coming from within, and since there was no actual platform on the end on which to ride, they were only able to use it for cover long enough to get to one of the tunnels. For this reason, their choice was made for them and once out of sight of the Kaiserhof platform they found themselves on the way to Friederichstraße.

They stumbled down the tracks as quickly as they could what with only the barest of light coming from the car ahead, until after what seemed forever, they reached the next platform.

There were far fewer civilians here, but they were no less bedraggled and vacant-eyed.

That is, until they saw Rolf's uniform, and then mouths turned down into frowns and eyes narrowed to slits, at least for those who felt the need to look at him at all. Ardell almost felt sorry for him—his father had always been hard to read;

'inscrutable' his mother had described him when she had still been with him and had been inclined to excuse his seeming aloofness, but 'disconnected' or 'incomprehensible' may have been more accurate terms. There just was never any real telling what was going on inside the man's mind, or heart. But this time Ardell *could* tell something was getting to him, by the way his shoulders hunched, and the look on the man's face that could only be described as baffled, as if he just didn't understand the resentment. This in and of itself did absolutely nothing to mollify the civilians, and this is why Ardell felt bad for him. He was only making it worse for himself.

He can't really be that dense... could he? Ardell rolled it back and forth in his mind. No, Rolf had to understand why the civilians were angry and hurt. He was usually adequately capable of understanding people's reactions once they were explained, it just seemed he couldn't do it on the fly. So the look on his face had to be something else.

Maybe he just couldn't understand why he was the target of their ire when he hadn't been the one in charge of the war, or the death squads, or any of the other sickening things Ardell had heard from the front. *That* he could understand Rolf feeling. He knew why Rolf had joined the army, he knew how his father felt about his homeland and its people, and he could full well imagine Rolf being caught flat-footed at being the one catching blame just because of a uniform.

Still, there was always the should-have-known-better clause.

"Hey!" Galya's voice cut through his train of thought and left it boarding at the station.

"Hey, what?" Ardell wasn't shy about letting the irritation show in his voice. He felt he had just had a special moment trying to understand his father. It had caught him off guard and he wasn't prepared to follow up on it, and now it was gone.

"Which way?" She was pointing at several branching tunnels ahead.

Ardell looked at Rolf, who was studying each one in turn in the dim light.

"I don't know which one to take," the older man grumbled. "That's the only one heading north, and it looks locked."

Galya stepped back and lifted one of the candles from a hole in the wall, engendering a foul look from its claimant that she had to quiet with a reassuring hand. She brought it close to the door, a massive steel affair secured with heavy chains and a padlock that looked as if it had been liberated from Neuschwanstein itself.

Something glittered on the cold metal and Ardell reached out a hand. He dabbed his fingers in it and held them to his nose, then his tongue.

"It's water. It's leaking water." He turned back to the disgruntled woman hunched under the place the candle had been. "Excuse me, ma'am. These doors, do you know where they go?"

"Do I look like I work for the *Reichbahn?*" she groused and huffed her shawl up around her neck and turned away, the very picture of indignation.

"Good point," Ardell conceded, and looked around more. Not far away he saw a middle-aged man with an empty sleeve pinned to his side, wearing a rumpled military-style service cap adorned with dual braids on the visor. *He does.*

Ardell stepped up and squatted in front of him. "Sir? These doors—"

"They go under the river!" He folded his one arm over his chest and turned toward the wall, mimicking the woman's attitude. "We seal them every night, in case there's a breach."

Even in the candlelight Ardell could see Galya pale. "I heard Meyer say Weidling had wanted to flood the tunnels to keep the Russians from using them."

Rolf took the candle and started examining the edge of the doors more closely. "I can't see that they're rigged to blow..."

Ardell left the railroader to his pique and rejoined the other two. "Even if they're not, with all the shelling..."

Galya looked around the station. "There would be no getting away."

Rolf set his jaw and replaced the candle. "Then it's time to cross overland."

Galya looked at Rolf as if he had finally lost his mind and it wasn't a surprise. "You think it's safe?"

Gruff voices echoed from far away, and as one of the three turned to look back down the tunnel they had come. Flashlight beams were stabbing the dark and the sound of booted feet on steel rails drifted to their ears.

Ardell looked from Rolf to Galya and back. "Safer than what? I say we go up, Fengeler won't be expecting that!"

"For good reason!" Galya countered.

Rolf huffed. "It's settled. This way." He waved them toward the broad stair leading to the surface station above.

Ardell paused only long enough to call out to the railroader, "By the way, you might want to lose that cap!"

XII

LIKE SO MANY other structures in Berlin the Friederichstraße station had once been a marvel of German engineering and style. Vaulted glass ceilings had arced high over the train platforms like a giant's Victorian greenhouse, but now most of that lay shattered on the tile floor, along with fallen steel frames and braces.

Rolf led the way as they stepped quickly from the stairs toward the north end of the building.

"Ssst!" he called suddenly, freezing in place. Just audible over the warfare and fires raging just blocks away booted feet on tile echoed through the huge space. "Get down!"

They scrambled for cover amid the benches, discarded luggage, and detritus of the siege as Fengeler, the proverbial bad penny, emerged from below.

With excited shouts the boys fanned out, flashlights playing carelessly across the ruin. Ardell bit his lip as his knees scraped across glass shards and broken concrete, and he wondered with a bit of a crazy mental chuckle if that new tetanus vaccine he had been 'encouraged' to take last year was really doing its job.

Tracers lanced through the blackness from the northwest and the excited babble turned angry.

"Get down!" Fengeler barked. "Put out those lights!"

A flashlight bounced across the rubble and came to rest shining on Ardell's face as he lay beneath a bench, but before he could slither back into the dark its owner dropped to the ground alongside, slack-jawed and glassy-eyed.

He scooted back a little faster until he reached Rolf and Galya. "Is there a better way out of here?"

"Pick a wall," Rolf whispered caustically, "but I'm going this way," and he continued toward the north end.

By the time they reached one of the windows overlooking the Spree the shooting had stopped. Ardell risked a look over the sill. "Too dark to see. Do we risk it?"

Near the center of the building gravel scraped faintly as Fengeler and his boys began to regroup.

Galya shrugged. "How else are we getting out?"

Ardell nodded and lifted himself over the threshold, but at that moment a screaming streak of smoke struck the wall not ten feet away and he fell to the ground, unconscious.

Ardell came to with Galya leaning over him, dabbing his face with what he supposed was what was left of someone's lingerie. In any case it was pink and lacy. "Ah, you're back!" She actually sounded relieved.

"How long was I out?"

"Maybe ten minutes."

"What was that?" He looked around anxiously. They appeared to be in a shell crater outside the station, but he couldn't see the river. Looking up didn't help, either. Peering through the smoke and glare from fires on every hand he was pretty sure the cloud cover that had hung over the city during the day was still present.

"*Panzerschreck,*" Rolf answered. "How do you say, 'bazooka'."

Rolf was sitting on the other side of the crater with his back partly toward them, apparently comparing two things in his hands. There was a soldier's body hanging over the edge of the crater and Ardell was pretty sure it was the young man he had seen talking to Rolf before the breakout. There was another body just within the hole, dressed in the coarse green of Stalin's attackers.

Ardell had an odd feeling about what Rolf was up to. He edged closer and saw his father had that little plastic soldier he had been carrying around in one hand, and—of all things— what looked like another in his other hand.

He shook his head, mystified, and suddenly turned his thoughts to more urgent issues. "Hey! What about Fengeler? Where is he?"

"Don't know," Galya shrugged. "We seem to have successfully lost him."

Something was nagging at Ardell's thinking but he was still a little too fuzzy-headed to put his finger on it. Something... something... something just now, just since he woke up... not Fengeler, he's not a threat just now...

And then he had it. He stared at his father and narrowed his eyes.

As if he could feel it, Rolf turned and looked at him squarely. "You noticed."

"You mean that you explained a Panzerschreck in American terms?" He looked sideways at Galya, who was now watching Rolf like a predatory cat. *He knows,* Ardell realized. "When did you figure it out?"

Rolf shrugged as if it really didn't matter. "Just after we left the Chancellery. You called her by name to distract the sniper. But you called her 'Galya'."

Ardell tried to watch them both simultaneously. Galya's hand was drifting toward her boot and Rolf was watching her warily.

He frowned. He hated being backed up to a wall. "If I tell you what you want to know, will you let it be?"

"Still trying to control the situation?"

"Do you want to know or don't you?"

Rolf pursed his lips, then rubbed his face. "Just as you want, Ardell."

Ardell breathed a little easier. "She was NKVD. Soviet Secret Police."

"Was?" Ardell wasn't sure if Rolf was skeptical or if he was just repeating it back to make sure he had heard it right. But before he could try to assign some inflection to his father's monotone he was speaking again. "Will she turn us in?"

Now Ardell turned his full attention on Galya, who spared him the barest glance. "I doubt it?" he ventured. "She wants out, too."

Rolf looked pointedly at Galya and Ardell was sure this time he was only looking for confirmation.

Galya apparently thought so as well. She nodded, once, and lifted her hand away from her boot.

Rolf sighed, took a long look at the destruction around them, and shrugged. "Then I will just have to trust you." He peered over the lip of the crater and seemed to nod to himself. "Can you walk?"

"I can walk."

"Then let's go." He stood, helped his son to his feet, and turned away without looking back.

Rolf led the way up the street, hugging the shadows and trying hard to keep his attention on the shattered buildings on either hand. It was hard, though. When they had dragged Ardell into the crater he had tripped over Wolfgang's body and Rolf had suddenly been paralyzed with a rush of emotion he honestly had had a hard time decoding. Seeing the expression on Wolfgang's face, the dismay frozen there at the sudden, final realization of his own mortality, had brought unbidden a memory from when Rolf's son Dieter had been just a small child getting ready to go to school. *It had been just after Ilse had left, and Rolf had been confronting the very likely probability that he would spend the rest of his life alone and unwanted. "You're going to like school," Rolf had encouraged. "It will help you grow up into a big boy, like me, or your cousin Hans, or your brother Delly. Don't you want to be a big boy?" Dieter's answer had cut him to the core, though. "I don't want to be a big boy!" Dieter had cried. "Why not?" Rolf had asked, mystified. "Because," Dieter had sniffed. "Look at you! Big boys are sad!"*

If the boy had only known how right he had been. And now Rolf had an aching empty pit in his chest and wanted nothing more than to get back to Arpke and smile for his little boy.

All that stood between him and that, was an entire war.

It didn't help that, once they had reached some bit of safety at the bottom of the hole, they had found a fallen Soviet soldier as well and, going through his pockets for weapons, a flashlight or anything else useful, he had instead come across a tiny thing that had further chilled his soul.

The man had been carrying a toy soldier of his own.

Now Rolf had both trinkets in his pocket and his thoughts were tumbling down a sharp slope of painful awakening. He was seeing now that people were people, that these Reds that he had been seeing only as targets, only as interlopers, had also left behind someone precious to them, that they probably weren't going to ever see again. At least it was brutally true for the poor soul in the crater. This man, this *father*, had gone to war because his home had been attacked. Yes, perhaps his leaders had brought him to this against his will, had helped inflict the indignity of the losses in the Great War on Rolf's home, but this nameless Russian had had nothing to do with that. In fact, the man looked Asian, and was probably a Mongol from the easternmost edges of Stalin's reach. He had most likely been conscripted into the fight, but then had seen the horror of the Eastern Front and, maybe then, had decided it was something he himself needed to put a stop to.

And then there was Wolfgang Schenk, no more than a boy, who had been deluded by fanatics like Fengeler into thinking this was all worth dying for, rather than realizing the futility of it all and trying to salvage something to rebuild after.

Rolf watched the ruins towering over him but now he was not just seeing potential perches for snipers. He was not just feeling the outrage of the brutality of Zhukov's advance. He was seeing the dashed hopes and dreams of individual men in shabby green uniforms massed together to throw themselves into this butcher's palace. He was seeing this as a destruction his own leaders had been just as eager to bring down upon all of them, as the Reds had been to deliver it. He had believed in the Party, had believed in its mission to help the people, but clearly now at the end the Party felt its mission was more important than anything else, even those same people they supposedly cared so much about.

He looked back at his two companions. Ardell seemed angry, no surprise there, but he also seemed to be watching Galya as if he were suspicious. He wondered if he should be concerned at this point, and realized with a start he was just too... too *something* to care. He wasn't really sure exactly what he was feeling, but something was replacing the normal survival instinct. If she were to stab him in the back, would it really be that bad? He had tried all his life to look after the people around him, not that they ever seemed to realize that. He looked back at Ardell again, determinedly watching his footing as he angled from shadow to shadow. Rolf had never understood why all his efforts to connect with his son had been rebuffed, time after time, or worse, just plain worked out so much worse than anyone could have expected, so he really *did* look like a worthless fool.

Could he really expect to do any better with Dieter, if he *did* get back to Arpke? Would Dieter even allow him to, as he got older? Or would he leave, like Margaret and Ardell? Like Ilse? He was suddenly overwhelmed with the thought of living out his final years in a shabby apartment, alone and forgotten, and grunted heavily to squash the emotion rising in his throat.

"What is it?" Galya asked.

Rolf turned around, momentarily confused as his mind raced for something to say, some excuse to hide what he had actually been thinking. Thankfully the universe seemed to take a moment's pity on him and he felt something wet on his face. He looked up. "Starting to rain. We should get inside again."

That seemed to satisfy her and they made their way into a nearby basement.

They descended the steps carefully and huddled at the bottom while their eyes adjusted to the even deeper black around them.

Galya gasped as she saw the woman crouching in the far corner. Another moment and it was apparent she had her arms protectively around two small girls. The three of them looked, as most of the civilians had, as if they hadn't bathed in days, and hadn't eaten in a good part of that time as well.

Rolf put his finger to his lips and spread out his other hand away from his body.

When this didn't seem to do anything to allay the woman's unease Galya laid a hand on Rolf's shoulder to stop him and stepped forward. "Excuse me, *Frau*. Have you seen any of our soldiers on this street?"

The woman glanced at Galya but then set her gaze squarely on Rolf. "A few," she spat, "running for their lives." She jutted her chin at Rolf. "You're the first officer."

Ardell stepped to Rolf's other side and squatted down on his heels. "What about the Russians? Any Reds in the area?"

The woman seemed marginally less distrustful of Ardell and sniffed, pointing a thumb over her shoulder. "They're all headed to the city center."

"They're not holding any positions here?"

"Just on the main streets."

Galya moved closer and knelt down next to the woman. "Then why are you still down here?"

There was a sneer in her voice that Rolf didn't need a light to see. "Women that go out are attacked."

Ardell was confused. "But if the Reds—"

"Not just the Reds!" Her reply was full of anger and clearly louder than she had intended, as she then hunkered back down and pulled her daughters in closer. Her eyes fixed on Rolf and didn't move. "*What's left of ours!*"

Rolf looked shocked, but an instant later seemed almost mournful. Ardell stood and pulled him back toward the stair. "Let's go. We're only going to attract attention here."

"Oh, I agree!" The gloating voice that answered from the top of the steps was only too familiar.

It was, of course, Fengeler. He slowly descended the steps, pistol drawn, and looked from Ardell to Rolf and back again. "Well! Look what we have here. My pair of deserters. You have proven to be quite the quarry!"

Galya slipped deeper into the basement and pulled the woman and her children with her.

Rolf noticed the movement out of the corner of his eye and started talking to distract Fengeler. "Have you looked outside? Do you have any idea of the military situation?

"I have indeed!" Fengeler confirmed. "I am very aware of the situation, as well as mindful of a flood of craven deserters and turncoats. Are *you* aware you are behind the Russian lines, Herr Captain?"

"Then you are as well."

Fengeler lifted his chin. "I have a mission."

"As do we. To escape, to have some hope of saving anything out of this wretched country when this is over."

"When this is over? My dear Captain! When this is over there will be no use in saving anything!"

Bile rose in Rolf's throat and the rage finally spilled out. "No use! *No use?* Is that what you've been telling those children that you've been leading around? The ones who've been dying for you? *Or the ones you were stringing up from every tree and lamppost on the Unter Den Linden?*"

"That's enough of that!" Fengeler raised his pistol to point between Rolf's eyes. "Take them upstairs! We will try this again!"

Once again Fengeler's youthful minions wrestled Rolf and Ardell to the ground.

Galya crawled out the basement window on the far side of the house and started purposefully down the street. Her choice of route was unimportant. She had heard what Fengeler had said about being behind the lines and it was a safe bet that a few blocks in any direction would get her what she needed.

She was not disappointed. A few hundred meters away she found a Soviet patrol working their way around a storefront. She reached into a pocket sewn into the waistband of her skirt, pulled out a small red leather wallet and flipped it open as she stepped up to the men.

"Comrades!" she called, brandishing the wallet.

The patrol stopped, stared for a moment, and closed eagerly on her. One large brute shouldered his way to the front of the gaggle and reached out as if he would grab her hair.

She deflected his grasping hand with a lightning-quick stroke and followed it up with an arm lock that flipped him around onto the ground. "*Nyet!*" she shouted at him.

The rest of the patrol stepped back, bringing rifles to bear, but she fixed them with an indignant glare and held her wallet up higher. "NKVD!"

It took all of about a second and a half for her words to register, then the patrol leader's eyes went wide. He shouldered his papasha and cautiously walked up to peer at the wallet.

His eyes, if possible, got even bigger. "Comrade Agent! Excuse us, please!" He turned back to his patrol and waved their weapons down, then kicked irritably at the first soldier. "Get up, you! Get back in line!" The man scrambled sheepishly to his feet and dusted himself off as he waved away the chiding of his fellows.

The patrol leader turned back to Galya and raised his hands in supplication. "Apologies, Comrade Agent! The men, they have been fighting for days—"

"Apologies?" Galya's tone was blistering. "Is this how you have been treating the women? Are you trying to turn the populace against us even more? You do realize when this is over, we will be ruling here? Or at least trying to?"

"Yes, Comrade Agent." The patrol leader was clearly torn between soothing the offended NKVD agent before him and not looking like a complete *slabak* to his men behind. "We are sorry, Comrade Agent."

"I agree! Undisciplined pigs! Now see here—I have two prisoners that were retaken by the Fritzes as deserters. I need to get them back so I can escort them to the rear."

The patrol leader seemed immensely relieved to have a hands-on task before him he could handle.

"Of course, Comrade Agent! At once!"

Rolf and Ardell stood before Fengeler in what had once been a kitchen. The SS Colonel leaned against the counter and read from a sheet on his clipboard.

"Captain Rolf von Heydn, Waffen-SS, lately commander of the 11th Panzergrenadier Division 'Nordland', and Jacob Klugmann, agent of the Geheime Staatspolizei. You are accused of deserting in the face of the enemy." He looked up at them with a bemused smile. "How do you plead?"

Ardell looked around at the shattered tile, the dry fixtures, the joists poking out of the broken ceiling, and the young but grim boys leveling weapons at them. Thankfully Galya was nowhere to be seen. "Um, not guilty?"

Fengeler seemed unimpressed. "Of course, you do. Nevertheless, evidence I have indicates the contrary."

"What evidence is that?"

Fengeler ignored him and pulled the paper off the clipboard to shove it into his bulging rucksack. "I hereby pronounce you guilty of desertion and impose the sentence of death by hanging." He nodded once to the oldest lad, who eagerly snatched up ropes and set to work. They dragged the two men outside to a solitary lamppost and settled nooses around their necks. With a flourish they tossed the bights over the post's crossbar and heaved them kicking into the air.

Gunfire erupted around them as Galya's patrol appeared.

The Nazis scattered, returning fire recklessly as they dove for cover. Fengeler, on the other hand, stood calmly in the building's entry, plinking at the Soviets with his pistol until they too dropped into safer positions.

Galya circled around to one side toward the lamppost and the patrol leader waved a fire team into a flanking position. "You two! Down there! Cover Comrade Agent!"

By this time Fengeler had exhausted his pistol ammo and tossed it aside. He collected a rifle from one of his fallen men and resumed firing as if he were at a carnival.

Galya took the chance offered by Fengeler's change of weapons to dash to the post. She whipped out her boot knife as she ran and with two quick strokes had Ardell and Rolf on the ground.

Their squirming struggles caught Fengeler's eye and he spun, firing, hitting Galya in the thigh, but with his attention diverted the Russians were able to intensify their attack and they were able to drive him back into the building.

Galya gritted her teeth and crawled closer to the two men until she could cut the bindings on their wrists. Ardell flung off his noose, snatched up a rifle and took off at a low crouch toward Fengeler's escape, but by the time he reached the building the man was gone.

It took a few moments longer for Ardell to realize the shooting had stopped. When the relative silence finally registered, he slowly looked around the street at the corpses littering the rubble, and all he could do was shake his head.

Galya was dressing her wound with the help of the patrol leader and pulled herself up by his coat sleeve. "Thank you, Sergeant. I have it from here."

The patrol leader looked at Rolf, still sitting under the lamppost rubbing his neck and gagging, and then at Ardell with his rifle. "Are you sure, Comrade Agent? There is only one of you, and—" He fell silent when he turned back to her and saw the look in her eye. Seemingly realizing there was much more to this situation than he knew or had rank or inspiration to deal with, he pulled himself up to his full height and cleared his throat. "Yes, of course, Comrade Agent! I see you have this firmly under control. Here," he handed her his own pistol and waved his men into line behind him. "Good luck!" He turned and led his men trudging on down the street to resume their push southward.

Galya turned and stopped when she saw Ardell looking at her. Whatever she saw on his face clearly puzzled her because her brow furrowed. "What?"

"I have to admit that I'm surprised to see you."

Galya let out a nervous half-chuckle. "Why?"

"I thought for sure you were gone. That you'd leave us behind, let Fengeler deal with me, since I—" he stopped and looked carefully at Rolf, but the other man was not paying attention. "—since I was your only witness."

"Oh, ye of little faith!" she quipped, then cocked an eyebrow at him. He nodded confirmation, and she continued, but with a sigh. "To be honest, Delly, I thought about it. But there was one thing..."

Ardell drew a deep breath, not sure what was coming next but pretty sure he wasn't going to like it. "One thing? Which was?"

"I've really come to respect you over the years, and, well, there was the whole thing in Dresden. I didn't want you to go without having a chance to set yourself straight."

"Set myself straight? What are you talking about?"

She looked him squarely in the eyes, and then slowly turned to look to Rolf. He turned as well, as she spoke as softly as the shooting a few blocks away would allow.

"I'm never going to see my father again. I'm never going to have a chance to make things right with him. Mostly that's my choice, and so I've made peace with it, but that doesn't make it hurt any less. Partly because I'm still going to miss my papa... and partly because I know what it's going to do to him." She stepped up and laid a hand on Ardell's cheek, turning his face back toward hers, and looked intently into his eyes. "I didn't want you to find yourself in the same place, Delly. One of us here is bad enough."

He had been right. He didn't like it.

XIII

D AWN WAS still some time away as they got back
underway. Without a backwards glance they left the
Friederichstraße station and its surrounding shopfronts and
apartments behind and started making their way up the gently
sloping street toward the Weidendammer Bridge.

It took a good while to get to the point they could see over
the crest of the rise, given the condition of the men after their
run-in with Fengeler. The emotional toll on all three of them
had been exhausting as well, and they still had to keep an eye
out for patrols from either side who were still trading fire just
one or two streets away. Fengeler had said they were behind
the Russian lines, but it seemed they only had passed the
actual front and were still within the main battle zone. The
streets were dark, the shells of buildings more so, glare of fires
just out of sight made seeing in the shadows that much harder,

and the low clouds reflected only enough of the ruddy light to give the scene an infernal hue.

Finally, they were able to peer over the slope at what they really were hoping would be their last obstacle on the way out of the tightening Soviet ring once and for all.

They were severely disappointed in the view that greeted their eyes.

The bridge itself was clear, but a tank ditch had been dug across the street at the far end with only a small gap in the center to allow passage. Whether it had been created by the Russians or the Germans was anyone's guess but in any case the Soviets were using it to full advantage—a heavy tank proudly bearing a red star and a slogan boldly picked out in large Cyrillic letters was digging in next to the shattered hulk of another, and a machine gun nest had been set up alongside as well. The wrecked first tank had apparently done its job well enough, though, as the ditch was littered with the burned-out carcasses of an armored halftrack, a Tiger tank, and a mobile AA gun that had all tried to break through and failed.

"Oh," Galya observed with some resignation. "We aren't getting through that!"

She got an odd feeling when she didn't get a response right away and turned to see Rolf looking squarely at her, his normally severe expression only a wooden mask. "What is it?" she asked, genuinely curious.

Rolf took another moment to answer, as if he were unsure how to proceed. "Can I ask? How do you know my son?"

Galya's lip turned to a sympathetic curl. "He was my partner, in Dresden."

Before Rolf could say anything else Ardell joined them. "You two done talking about me? Wow!" His eyes grew wide at the sight at the far end of the bridge. "We aren't getting through that!"

Galya blew a tendril of hair from her face. "Yes, we decided that already."

"Is there another way across?"

"There's a small rail bridge a few hundred meters west," Rolf offered listlessly.

Ardell looked to the left where Rolf was pointing. There was a catwalk there, sure enough, but... "That thing? It looks awfully exposed. And how would we get there? It's all open on this side of the station, we'd be sitting ducks. We'd have to circle all the way around the south of the station. That would take us over an hour in these conditions and that's getting us too close to dawn."

"But the Reds hold everything further west, and there's nothing left to the east that we can reach." He looked to their right where the remains of the Ebertsbrücke lay in the water where sappers had blown it days before.

Suddenly Rolf stood up slightly and cocked an ear.

"What is it?" Galya whispered.

Rolf furrowed his brow and held up his hand for quiet, then pointed vaguely toward the tank trap.

Over the waves of belligerence echoing from all sides could be heard the faint sounds of singing.

Rolf held his breath. Sure enough, he was catching a ragged masculine chorus. In Russian, of all things. He pondered this for a moment, dumbfounded, and studied the soldiers digging the tank in as best he could. They seemed to be passing around a bottle and were moving rather unsteadily.

Then realization struck him. He slid back from the crest. "The rail bridge won't be a problem. The Reds are tired... and drunk."

"Drunk?" Galya was surprised, and Rolf in turn was amazed she was. "Why would they be drunk?"

"Don't you know what day it is?" he prompted.

She counted out days on her fingers and her eyes lit up. "It's May Day!"

Rolf nodded resolutely. "It's May Day." He stood and dusted himself off. "We need to get moving. We still should stay to the south of the station, and you're right, Ardell, it's going to take us time to circle round." He turned back down the street and nearly walked into a young soldier who had come up behind him, beaming.

It was Eemi.

"Sir!" The relief in the young man's voice was clear, even to Rolf. "Sir, you're still alive!"

"Eemi?" was all Rolf could manage.

"I'm so happy I found you!" Eemi covered his mouth and it seemed for a moment his eyes were tearing, though Rolf admitted that may have only been the pervading smoke hanging in the air.

"Eemi..." Rolf wasn't sure what to do. Part of him wanted to hug his old radioman, but Eemi was, despite everything, still in uniform and professional decorum kept him rooted awkwardly in place. "Are... are you out here alone?"

"Oh, no, sir! There's more of the men just down the block." He pointed south, beyond where the three had left their shell hole. "We found the tanks, sir! We're getting ready to cross the bridge!" He gestured excitedly at the tank trap ahead. "Well, most of us, that is... the U-bahn... I don't know if you know..."

Rolf nodded and tried to put a reassuring tone in his voice. "I know, Eemi. To be honest, I'm surprised to find you here."

Eemi looked hurt. "I couldn't leave them, sir. I just couldn't."

Rolf shook his head. "I never realized you were that close to your crewmates. You always seemed more attached to your radios."

"Oh, not just them, sir. The civilians."

"The civilians? Which civilians?" There was an image in Rolf's mind of what the old man at Kaiserhof had said, about soldiers ditching their uniforms in favor of garb more suited to rats abandoning a sinking ship.

Something of that must have crept into his voice because Eemi squirmed uncomfortably. "Um... well, can you come with me, sir?"

Rolf looked to Ardell and Galya for some insight into what to expect but they seemed equally mystified. He turned back to the young private. "By all means. Lead on."

Eemi led them a few blocks back down the street to an alley shrouded in deep shadow.

After a few moments Rolf could make out a line of vehicles—four or five of Rolf's old halftracks and three Tigers, each bearing a different divisional insignia. The men manning them were his, though, but the more startling sight was the several dozen Berliners clustered around, in, and over the machines. Oldsters, young mothers, children large and small, united by their facial expressions of fatigue mixed with a final, faint glimmer of hope.

Eemi turned a much more expectant look on him. "We have to get them across the bridge, sir. If we can make it that far, we can get them out of the city."

Rolf heard the unasked question. He despised unasked questions, the mathematician in him much preferred to have things out in the open where there could be no assumptions. "But?" he prompted.

"But we're a few men short. We need you, sir! We need you to command one of the panzers. Then we can use all three. Then we'll stand a chance!"

Rolf pondered this for a moment, working out the lineup in his head, along with approach speeds, visibility, and what he knew was just a guess at the actual fuel left in any of the tracks.

Apparently Eemi mistook Rolf's silence for hesitation. "Sir? You saw what happened when they tried to cross with only one tank."

Rolf nodded in agreement, recalling the charred hulks cluttering the far end of the bridge. He took a deep breath and thought hard about his answer.

Ardell caught his breath as well, but when Rolf glanced at him, he could see it was for an entirely different reason. His son was staring at one of the halftracks... no, he was staring at one of the refugees in particular, propped up against the road wheel and drinking from a water bottle held by an old woman.

Fengeler.

His usually immaculate uniform was in disarray, with tunic unbuttoned and shirt stained with sweat and grime. His eyes were empty as well, as if he wasn't even aware of his surroundings, and the way the woman had to wipe his face after giving him the drink appeared to confirm that.

Rolf shook his head. He'd seen this enough in the past year. He swept his eyes over the tanks, their *zimmerit* coatings patched and streaked from dust, ash and rain, and the halftracks with their motley of human misery.

Yes. I'd seen enough.

He turned and walked over to Galya, and without a word pulled Dieter's toy soldier out of his pocket and handed it to her. She took it, surprised, but then her lips set in a grim line and she nodded to him. Her eyes, though, looked almost pleading.

Rolf chose not to answer and turned away quickly. "Eemi!" he called.

"Sir?"

"Get the civilians in the tracks."

Ardell was stunned. "Get them in the—Are you *nuts?* Didn't we just decide there was no getting across that bridge?"

Rolf regarded Ardell with his typical stony expression, but when he spoke his voice was uncharacteristically gentle.

"Are you suggesting trying to get them over the rail bridge? On foot? A lot of these people are injured. And those that aren't... Just look at them." He waved a hand over their fearful faces. "They're in no condition to walk it."

"That's not what I mean..." Ardell's voice, in turn, was becoming defensive, and he didn't like it. He wasn't used to his father being... *sympathetic.* "Going over by the street is sure to get us all killed! All of them killed!"

Rolf pursed his lips. "No. We have three Tigers."

"And they have a T-34 and probably twenty panzerfausts they took from your own people! This is madness!"

"Perhaps it is," Rolf conceded, "but what else can I do? Would you have me just leave them here?"

"No, but... but..." Ardell sputtered. "What about Fengeler? Does he even deserve to go?"

Rolf's voice started to wind up a more typical irritated edge. "No, he doesn't." He looked Ardell in the eye. "But that's not for me to decide."

"Oh, you're just going to leave it to the Fates, is it? Why isn't it for you to decide? You're the one with the tank!" Ardell crossed his arms and scowled. "Why are you throwing your life away for this lost cause? You were such a smart man! The smartest man I knew! How could you not know this would come to this?" He waved his hands in a large circle, encompassing all of the destruction around him. "And I don't mean just this here, to be clear! I mean the whole Nazi thing!"

Rolf shook his head tiredly. "No one saw this coming, Ardell. Not at the beginning."

"*Mom* did. But you wouldn't listen. You just couldn't stand to displease your party masters!"

"Now just stop right there!" Now Rolf was shouting, and his face, even for him, was livid. "I *never* said the Party was perfect! I *never* said they were the answer to *everything*. What I said was that they had answers to our problems of the day. The inflation, the unemployment, the factions roving the streets breaking windows—"

"They were the ones breaking windows!"

"They weren't the only ones!"

"Pah! There's no talking to you!"

"Because you're not talking! You're dictating! You're telling me what I was thinking, like you knew better than me what was in my own head!"

"Well, I never knew what was in your head! I still don't!"

"And yet you sure don't have a problem telling me what you're sure is in there!"

Ardell gritted his teeth. *This is getting us nowhere.* "I don't know what's wrong with you, *Dad*, I really don't! Trying to run that bridge, even with *three* tanks... it's just suicide! There's no chance you're going to get through that!"

"And why do you care?" Rolf scowled, balled his fists and shoved them in his pockets. "Why do you *really* not want me to go, Ardell? *Why?* Aren't you finished with me yet? Haven't got your full pound of flesh? Not quite done twisting the knife?"

"Now that isn't fair!"

"When was this ever *fair?* When, Ardell? *When?*"

They glared at each other for several long moments. Ardell was boiling inside by now. *The nerve!* It left him speechless. *Who the hell does he think he is? Twisting the knife! After the way he's been? The way he's always been?* He stared into his father's eyes, trying to read those dark pools.... Normally they were either blank as a fresh canvas, or stern as a schoolmaster's, but this time they were actually... hurt. Ardell was amazed at the pain he suddenly saw, and in the end, he wasn't able to hold the gaze.

Rolf took a deep breath, pulled his fists out of his pockets and clutched them together tightly. He stepped up close, and when he spoke the anger was gone, replaced by contrition. "Really, Ardell, what do I have left? All I ever tried to do was make things better for those around me." His hands fell to his sides and he seemed to sag. "And yet here I am. Here *we* are. Did I make good choices? They seemed so at the time, but now?" He looked around at the burned-out buildings and the battered civilians, and took a deep breath of the smoke-laden air. "Not nearly so much."

Ardell thought there was a crack in his voice and strained to see his expression in the dim light, but couldn't be sure what he found.

Rolf drew a shaky breath. "In the end, I'm just a man." He shrugged and dropped his hands tiredly to his sides again. "I'm just a man. Who made mistakes."

Over his shoulder Ardell saw Galya trying dramatically to get his attention. He threw her a questioning look and she nodded toward Rolf intently.

But Rolf hadn't noticed Ardell's shift in attention and was still speaking, as if to the world at large, looking everywhere and nowhere at once. "I'm just as human as anyone else. Don't I get to have regrets? Don't *I* get to see my sins and ask for forgiveness? Don't *I* get a chance to change, to make restitution? Your mother hasn't spoken to me in ten years." There was a definite hitch in his voice now. "You and I see each other for the first time since you were a boy and your first words are thrown at me like I'm some kind of beast. My leadership thinks I'm a traitor." He looked back at Fengeler, and then the cowering civilians. "Even my own people spit on me. What have I got left? Nothing. *Nothing.*"

He sighed deeply and it was another long moment before he spoke again. "But I keep going. I keep trying. Do you *really* want to know why, Ardell? Do you really want me to tell you, instead of you just assuming you know? Because you don't." He looked his son in the eye again and Ardell was surprised to see he appeared on the verge of tears. "It's not because I'm blindly devoted to some ideology. I've seen enough in the last year to put *that* to rest. Whether you choose to believe me or not, it's all I know how to do. I don't know how *not* to keep going. And look around. Who will take them over, if not me? Who gets left with this, if I don't?" He took another deep breath, less shaky now. "Look, son... I hurt you. I know. You're right. I didn't know how to raise you. I didn't figure it out until Dieter came along and by then it was too late. You were gone. I'm sorry. I'm really sorry. For how I treated you, and the part I had in all... this. But I'm going to try to make things right. Even if..." He stopped and looked around again at everyone, soldiers and civilians, who were awkwardly transfixed at what they were witnessing. "Even if everyone here thinks I'm worthless. Every *single one* of us standing here right now."

Including himself. Ardell was angry still, but now for different reasons. Did his father really think he could get himself off the hook by trying to apologize now? After everything that had happened?

"Ardell, I'm going to leave it up to you. You can come with us and take your chances with odds on the most potent armored vehicle ever made. Or you can make for the rail bridge, and I'll wait until you're ready and then cross here as a diversion so they won't even notice you. Either way... I'm going over the bridge. I just want to be able to do something to get you home." He sighed deeply. "I only ask that you make your decision now. It's going to be dawn soon."

Now Ardell was stuck, trying to decide. Climbing into the halftrack was one thing, but crossing an exposed steel catwalk alone was another thing entirely.

Galya edged around Rolf, pausing only long enough to touch his shoulder and give him an understanding look. Ardell noted his father's expression in return was puzzled, as if he were trying to fit her reaction into a template he could make sense of. This was no surprise to Ardell, who had known for years his father always seemed to understand what people were trying to tell him only long after the fact.

She stepped up to Ardell and pulled his ear down to her lips. "Get in the track, Delly. You know there's more Reds to worry about than just the ones at the end of the bridge! And besides, he's trying to reach out to you."

"You tell me," Ardell's frustration was evident. "Is he really a penitent sinner? Or is he just playing for sympathy?"

She squinted at him as if he were dense. "Do you want to waste this opportunity to find out? If he's just playing, you'll know soon enough, but at least then you'll stand a better chance of being alive to gain satisfaction from ignoring him for the rest of your life!"

Ardell looked past her to Rolf, who was standing apart from everyone else, blowing out deep breaths and putting his hands in and out of his pockets as if he had no idea what to do with them. The young Eemi stood close by, watching his commanding officer with heartfelt concern, and for a moment Ardell felt guilty he couldn't bring himself to feel the same way.

Rolf looked up and Ardell's expression became flint. He shook himself loose from Galya's grip, stepped purposefully up to the ramp at the back of the lead halftrack and climbed in. Once aboard he stood up in the open rear compartment and watched, for the first time, his father actually in action.

It was quite a remarkable transformation, really. The man that only a moment before had appeared overwhelmed by his very life was standing tall, speaking and moving with supreme confidence, secure in his own environment. This effect was not lost on his men, either; Ardell saw the trepidation so evident in Eemi's face was gone and the young man was smiling as if order had been restored to the world.

Rolf fished in his tunic pocket for a cigarette pack, shook one out, frowned at the apparently now-empty box and tossed it aside. "The Tigers will lead," Rolf declared as he lit up, "and set the pace. We will pull out of the alley and stage just short of the rise in an echelon left formation. I will take the leftmost side. Gunter, you will take center, and Felix will lead on the right. This should keep the T-34 from seeing all three of us at once while we concentrate fire on him. Be loaded and ready. Once we crest the rise, we will need fifteen seconds to reach the trap and I want that tank taken out before we get there. Also! It's May Day, which means the Reds have been drinking." This got a bare chuckle from the crews.

"Their reflexes will be slowed and they shouldn't be able to get more than one round off in the time we'll be exposed."

Ardell was taken aback at this last comment. *One round could take out one Tiger. He basically just said we'll probably lose one of us, but that's acceptable.*

I'd say your odds are about one in three... Director Brenner's words dropped into Ardell's gut in a déjà vu so intense he could feel the 'fump' as it landed.

I am *the only guy you got for this job...*

Who will take them over, if not me?

Rolf now turned to Eemi and the other halftrack drivers. "The SPW's will make single file behind the center to break through the gap in the tank ditch once we've dealt with the defenses. Stay back thirty meters so Felix and I will have space to get in line as we go through, but don't get any farther back than that or they will have time to regroup and you'll be done for. Once we're on the other side we will spread back out and hang back to cover you from any survivors as Gunter leads you out of the city. Are there any questions?"

Seeing there were none, he waved them off and they separated to their vehicles.

Within moments the crews were in place, hatches were closed, and Rolf circled his hand over his head to signal the drivers to start their engines. Seeing all was as in order as it was likely to get, he carefully climbed up and into the command hatch of the second tank.

He offered each of his vehicle commanders a solemn hand-to-temple salute of the *Heer*.

He turned to face the end of the alley.

"*Ausfahren!*"

XIV

SASCHA SIMINOVITCH was feeling pretty good, all things considered. The battle had been a bloody and slow slog, for sure, getting through these damned streets that always felt like they were closing in on him. Things here in Germany were so different than back home on the steppes, where the land was wide and flat. Here there were hills everywhere, trees where there weren't hills, and in the city itself looming buildings that seemed to serve the same purpose—to make him feel like he was in a deadly bramble infested with hornets.

But that had been two weeks ago, when they had first moved into the suburbs. Sascha had been pretty sure then that he would never see the end of the fight, that it would drag on for months and end with him going back east in a box. As it was, though, they were actually on the verge of victory. The government quarter was literally in line of sight. The People's

Banner was flying over the Reichtag, and it was May Day! Since midnight his comrades had been dipping into the vodka rations, and now that the machine gun nest here was set, they were standing in a circle, passing around a bottle and seeing how fast they could drain it.

There was still heavy fighting going on to the southeast where the Reichtag sheltered a few holdouts that were stubbornly refusing to accept their fate, and the explosions, gunfire, and shouts and screams were carrying across the river and making it difficult to hear even his inebriated squadmates ten yards away. Sascha had a buddy somewhere over there and he worried he was all right.

The mood over here, though, was decidedly different. Since things *were* clearly getting close to the end Sascha had noticed some of the zeal had faded. At Seelow everyone had been frothing at the mouth to get their hands on German throats. Now, though, no one seemed to want to be the last to die for the cause.

He looked down the several streets feeding into the intersection, limited though his view was by darkness and smoke, and decided it would be safe to take a moment to join the drinking circle.

As he stepped off from the barricade there was a flash in the depths of the haze shrouding the south side of the river, and their tank went up like a Roman candle.

Rolf smiled in spite of himself. He was actually having a hard time identifying what he was feeling; he knew at least partly it was the satisfaction of a good plan well executed, but it was much more than that. If he had ever known real joy in his life, he might have labeled it that way. They were halfway across the bridge, escape was within reach, and the Russian tank had not even been a threat. *Felix had always had the best crew,* he reflected. His Number Two had obviously taken his advice to heart and had taken the shot as soon as his gunner had had line of sight.

And Rolf stood a real chance of doing something good for his oldest son at long last.

He keyed his throat mic. "Stand by to launch anti-personnel grenades." The *Sprenggranatparone* was a risky weapon to use in these circumstances. They only had a launch range of ten meters at best and a blast radius of a hundred, so shrapnel falling into the open-topped halftracks was a real risk, but he had already done the calculations on it and felt it wouldn't do anything more than frighten the civilians. But they needed to clear that machine gun nest. He didn't have confidence the halftracks' armor would stand up to it.

He counted seconds and watched the burning hulk of the T-34 draw closer in his periscope.

"Launch!"

There was a satisfying *foom!* from just off his right hand and a moment later the nest was nothing but a misty pink memory being raked over by his own gunners.

He sat back in his stool and grabbed hold of his hatch release, bracing himself for the vault through the trap.

Then the smoky arcs of captured panzerfausts started crisscrossing their path.

Ardell was no stranger to combat. He'd managed to encounter enough over the last years in his various roles, though he had never really been a front-line type. But this was nerve-wracking. The roar of the engines, the glow of the fires, the smoke, the dust, the screams and gunfire, all pointing to the knowledge that people who really wanted him dead were only a few feet away... it was really an entirely different world.

Then there was a huge blast that he felt in his gut and set the rest of the civilians to frightened shouts and wails. He was pretty sure he saw a turret doing somersaults off to their right and nearly stood to look.

"Get *down!*" Galya cried and clutched his jacket. "Are you insane?"

"What was that?" he yelled over the ringing in his ears.

"What do you think?" Her voice was muffled even though she was clearly shouting. "It was a Tiger!" Her eyes were wide and frightened. "Pray they don't have another round for us!"

The shock of Felix's track taking a direct hit battered Rolf's machine and rattled the men inside like dice in a cup. By the time Rolf got himself situated back on his seat he already knew what had happened, and there was nothing to do in the moment but envy that his Number Two had met his end the way he would have preferred.

He checked his periscopes to the right. As best he could tell through the thick glass Felix's machine had rolled to a stop on top of the nest and was spewing thick oily smoke that at least was able to provide them with some cover. There were still Russians here and there among the rubble trying to fire small arms, and there were still panzerfausts plowing their deadly trajectories, but most of these shots were going wild in the Reds' drunken hysteria and his column was able to push through without stopping.

Like clockwork his driver slipped in behind Gunter. To the rear, Rolf was relieved to see Eemi was goosing his halftrack to close the distance. He popped the hatch and stood for a better look. They were clear of the trap, all of them save Felix, poor bastard, and making good speed northward. He allowed himself a deep breath but caught it again when they roared through the Karlstraße intersection.

He checked down the left roadway, toward the Reichtag, and good thing, too—there was a massive column moving in their direction: a double row of T-34's and IS-2's with dozens of infantry. He wasn't sure if they were responding to his breakout or just lamentably happened to be on the move for their own reasons, but it didn't matter. That much firepower would make short work of the halftracks.

And they were crossing right in front of them.

"*LINKS!*" Rolf yelled.

His crew responded instantly. The driver dove for the northwest corner of the crossing and slammed to a halt in a narrow alley as the gunner slung the turret around with a speed that nearly unseated Rolf for a second time. The loader had already done his job, though, and the instant the driver reversed far enough for the gunner to get the lead Russian tank in his sights the other man fired without waiting for a command.

The loader was on his game and had another round in the breech within a heartbeat. The gunner adjusted his aim slightly to the left and fired again, and the deadly accuracy of the long eight-point-eight left another tank burning, effectively blocking the road.

Rolf turned to where his Number Three had slowed to see what was happening. "Go! Go! Go!" he yelled, waving furiously as his driver backed fully out of the alley to turn face toward the new threat so their machine gunner could take over.

Ardell had had enough. The rifle rounds pinging off the halftrack's armor as they had raced through the trap had stopped, but then there was a loud blast just off to the left. This was no random, wild explosion, though, but rather the deliberately belligerent sound of a large-caliber round going downrange. Then Eemi hit the brakes, just for a moment, and he heard Rolf shouting something over and over as the engine slowed. He angrily shoved off Galya's clutching grasp and stood to look over the top of the armor plate.

They were passing through the next intersection and the Reds were advancing up the street a few hundred meters away. Trying to, anyway. The column was held up behind a brace of burning hulks. Men were swarming all around trying to get past them, and behind he could just make out other large shapes moving to clear positions.

Just to their own left Rolf's tank was backing out of an alley and spinning on its tracks as his father stood in his hatch, waving furiously at Gunter in the lead machine. There was a clatter of machine gun fire from Rolf's track and the Russians began scattering again.

All this he took in in an instant.

Rolf craned his neck around to check the rest of the column as Eemi sped past, but he stopped for just a moment as he locked eyes with his son. Ardell returned the gaze, not even aware of his own expression but at least registering some kind of... sadness in his father's eyes.

There was a muzzle flash from one of the blocked-in Soviet tanks down the street and the corner of the building next to Rolf burst into concrete chips and dust as the edifice collapsed into a heap.

The last thing Ardell was able to see as the dust billowed was Rolf shielding his face from the onrushing wave of debris, and then Eemi was gunning the engine again as he dodged around the Orainenberger Tor onto Müllerstraße and they left it all behind.

Epilogue

WHEN THE SUN finally rose the smoke and dust hanging in the air mingled with the morning fog to make a thick, oppressive blanket over the suffering of the city. The skies were quiet, as the night fighters had retired and the day bombers and Shturmoviks would not be able to get a start until the mists burned off.

On the northern verge of the city the bulk of the Humboldthain flak tower squatted on a low rise just above the pall. Ground activity had been quiet here as well, as the Soviets had determined days before the structure was too heavily built and too well defended to waste effort upon, when the Reichtag, the Chancellery, the Gestapo Headquarters, and other very symbolic targets, were going to be much easier to take down and were just a little further onward.

For this reason, those fleeing the city center who managed to make it to the tower had been quite surprised to see fresh troops in pressed uniforms ranged on its battlements and patrolling its grounds. By the same token the tower's denizens, largely immune to the horrors raging a few kilometers away and only knowing of them by report, were stunned at actual sight of the ragged desperation they saw crawling out of the mists.

So it was as a young guard stepped forward to meet the survivors of Rolf's column and confer briefly with Gunter's tank. He pointed to a sandbagged revetment not far away where the Tiger's firepower could be put to use, and then walked up to Ardell's machine as Eemi opened the rear hatch and the haggard civilians climbed out to stretch their legs on their way to relieving their bladders, or their stomachs, in the trees.

"Private!" one of the guards called to Eemi. He was eyeballing the Nordland Division badge on the fender and his eyes were wide. "Did you come from the Citadel Sector?"

Eemi nodded. "We did. Hey! Do you have any fuel?"

"We do, as a matter of fact." He turned and waved to one of his counterparts near the door who slipped back inside.

He turned back to Eemi. "What did you think of General Bärenfänger's relief attack?"

Ardell wandered closer to listen in. Eemi was shaking his head at the other man. "There was a counterattack?"

The guard looked genuinely puzzled. "There was... the general left here a few hours ago with tanks and infantry. He was supposed to punch through to the Reichtag, open a corridor. I figured that's how you got out."

Ardell shook his head at the young man's hopefulness. "The Reichtag is gone. So is the Chancellery, and all the rest. The fighting has nearly stopped."

"Surely you must have seen something, sir? It was a sizable force."

Ardell shook his head again. "I'm sorry. We've seen nothing. By the way, has anyone else been through here? Maybe a Tiger? Other Nordlanders?"

The guard pondered. "Nordland? No, sir. Not long after midnight General Mohnke came through with a few others, but that's all we've seen."

By then a bucket brigade had formed to bring out jerry cans to the halftracks. As they started refueling Ardell walked a short distance away to get a better look at the city.

The destruction was nearly everywhere and worse than when he had parachuted in just a few days before, but bizarrely there were still neighborhoods here and there that appeared relatively untouched. Not so the center, though, where only shattered remnants of buildings that had been at one time beautiful, imposing, or both, poked up through the mists.

The routes into the city told the tale, though—choked with seething masses of bright olive green flowing around hulking massive beetle-like tanks. The river of Soviets into the wreckage seemed endless.

And nothing was heading outward.

A whistle sounded behind him. He turned to see the fuelers collecting their cans and heading back into the tower and his riding companions climbing back into the tracks. He must have been longer than he'd thought, pondering the death of Berlin.

He swept his eyes one last time over the remains of the city, turned, and headed back to take his seat.

By evening they had reached the River Elbe. Eemi had managed to rescue some bedsheets from a large house along the way and these had been strung along the flanks of the halftracks as makeshift white flags once they were safely out of the Soviet zone.

The checkpoint itself was a sprawling affair of tents and muddy paths and swarmed with civilians being marshaled into processing lines by dour soldiers with 'MP' cuffs on their sleeves. Eemi led his line to a parking field and lined up with dozens of other vehicles of all descriptions—halftracks, autos, horse-drawn wagons, trucks, even some of those uniquely

German tracked-motorcycle hybrids. He pulled up to a halt under the careful guidance of another MP, shut his engine down once and for all, and dropped his face into his hands. Ardell was fairly certain he saw the boy's shoulders quiver like he was crying, but after a moment Eemi took a deep breath, rubbed his face, and climbed out after the rest of his charges.

They queued up in sullen files at the processing tables where those who had papers had them checked, those who didn't tried to explain who they were, and then photos were taken and new documents were filled out to the best of the ability of admin NCO's who were obviously dealing with significantly more work than they had been prepared for. As each individual reached the end of the journey, they were handed a fresh set of temporary papers and directed to the mess tents where they would finally get a hot meal and a blanket.

Ardell had stepped out of line early and flagged a senior MP to hand over his actual identification that he had kept hidden in the lining of his jacket. This had, as he had expected, been met with some skepticism which Ardell couldn't blame the man for, and he was waiting patiently for the ponderous wheels of the OSS to turn and confirm his identity once the MP could manage to place a call back to London.

He stood with one shoulder propped up against the tent pole, scowling and replaying his last moments with Rolf over and over in his head.

Suddenly Galya appeared at his elbow. She had a crisp white typewritten paper in one hand and Rolf's little toy soldier in the other. "Delly, you look horrible! What's wrong?"

When Ardell spoke, his voice came out a lot more bitter than he was intending. "He waited until the last minute to say anything. Ten years! And he waits until we're charging across a bridge into a Russian trap." He blew out a heavy breath. "It's just typical."

Galya's response was not sympathetic. "Delly! Let me make sure I have this right. You finally get the apology you waited years for, and you're complaining... because of the *timing?*"

The edge in his voice sharpened. "But what am I supposed to do with it? Now *I* look like the asshole because I didn't say anything back to him."

"Well, you *are* the asshole, but it's not because you didn't answer him."

That didn't help Ardell's mood in the slightest. "You care to explain that?"

"Oh, sure! I'll... draw you a map!" She smiled brightly at recalling the idiom right. "What you're worried about is how *you* look. But have you thought about what he *felt*? Maybe he didn't feel he *could* say anything to you any earlier. Judging by what you've told me and what I've seen for myself, you weren't welcoming at all since you've been here, and I can only imagine what your interactions with him must have been like with an ocean between you."

Ardell glared at her and wished she wasn't so good at this.

But she wasn't paying attention, or was choosing to ignore him. "Delly, please. Don't think that he waited to tell you this so you wouldn't have time to come up with an answer. Don't think that he held you off long enough so that he could make you look like a jerk. Maybe he did, I'll grant you that. But if you think of it like that you'll never get past this moment. Look at it this way. The fact that you had no time to reply is *not your problem...* it's his. Do you understand? He wanted you to know he was sorry... but he knew none of us might make it across the bridge, and he probably wouldn't have another chance to tell you. He'd let too many other chances go by, for whatever reason, and it was... now or never. It's not your fault he waited so long, it's his." She smiled again, more genuinely this time, laid a hand on Ardell's cheek, and whispered, "But at least he managed to get it out when it really mattered."

Ardell thought about that for a long moment. He had to admit her perspective helped a little, but he was still angry.

Then his mind lit up and he realized with a start that what he was actually angry about was that his father had the audacity to *not make it out of the city.* It's not like he planned it on purpose, Ardell knew, but nevertheless, it left him feeling like he had had an opportunity taken away. Not only had he lost his father, but he had lost whatever chance he would have had to finally make things right... and was just as surprised to find that, now that that chance was gone, he had really wanted it.

He stared at the slow lines of refugees as if he thought he might see Rolf's stern face among them. There was a slight shakiness in his voice when he finally spoke. "Do you think he made it out?"

Galya nodded. "I'm sure we will see him again. He's a smart trooper."

"Right, sure." His anger was subsiding, but his frustration was still there. "I don't know how we're ever going to find him in all this mess."

"Oh, don't worry about that, Delly." Now there was a knowing tone in her voice. "We don't have to find him. *He's* going to find *us*."

"He is? How?"

"Because, Delly, you and I are going to Arpke." She held up the little toy soldier. "We've got to look after your brother Dieter."

"'We'? How do you mean, 'we'? I thought you were going to slip off to Switzerland, fade into the background?"

Galya feigned outrage. "And leave you running around unattended, my only witness?" She held up the typewritten sheet. "Not a chance! You and me, Delly. *We're married.* Says so right here!"

It took a moment for Ardell to realize what she had done. "Ma—*married?*" he sputtered. "What are you—what possessed you to—"

Galya pressed a finger to his lips. "What was it I told you in the Chancellery?"

Ardell's mind raced, now thoroughly off kilter and looking for some sandy bottom to put its figurative feet on. "That there are some things that will be beyond my control no matter what I do?"

Galya laughed loudly and clapped her hand over her mouth. "Yes, that's true! But that's not what I'm talking about."

She eyed him expectantly and when he only stared blankly back, she sighed. "How about, 'keep your friends close, and your enemies closer'?"

Ardell frowned and sighed as well as he finished her thought. "Yeah... and family closest of all."

About The Author

Steve grew up on a farm in Northeast Ohio where he spent his free time reading Burroughs, Lovecraft, Zelazny and Tolkien, and his earliest writing efforts were creating adventures for his Dungeons & Dragons group. A veteran of the Army and the Navy, he currently lives near his childhood hometown. He has won awards for his writing in collaboration with Michael Eging on *The Silver Horn Echoes: A Song of Roland*, and has, with Mike, previously published *The Paladin of Shadow Chronicles: Volume One, Annwyn's Blood*, and *Volume Two: Ash and Ruin*.

also available from **TAYLOR & WELLS**

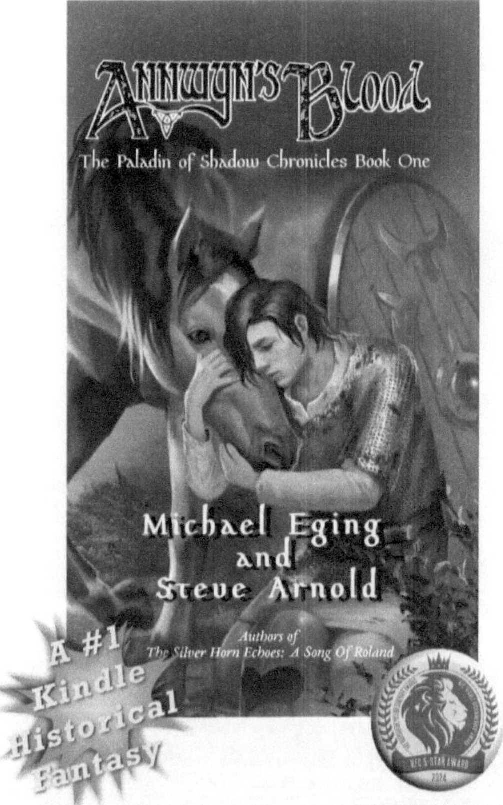

A #1 Kindle Historical Fantasy

"A fantastic read... its pacing is perfect, the characterization intuitive, and the style is perfect for the dark setting."
Stuart Kenyon, author of the
Augmented series

Available now on

amazon

www.ingramcontent.com/pod-product-compliance
Lightning Source LLC
Chambersburg PA
CBHW032030310726
48972CB00002B/604